A RAGE WITHIN

Also by March Hastings

Abnormal Wife
Again and Again
The Boys of Brigham Dee
By Flesh Alone
Crack-Up
The Demands of the Flesh
Design for Debauchery
Enraptured
Fear of Incest
The Heat of the Day
Her Private Hell
The Jealous and Free
Obsessed
The Outcasts
A Rage Within
Savage Surrender
The Soft Way
Three Women
The Third Sex
The Third Theme
The Unashamed
Veil of Torment
Whip of Desire

A RAGE WITHIN

MARCH HASTINGS

CUTTING EDGE

ISBN-13: 978-1-957868-21-9

Published by
Cutting Edge Books
PO Box 8212
Calabasas, CA 91372
www.cuttingedgebooks.com

CHAPTER ONE

She heard the egg cup hit the wall behind her and the splinter of porcelain shattering easily against white washed brick. Disgust smeared over her face like the yolks running down the wall. She got the sponge, as she always did, and went to wipe up the mess, holding her silence aloof from him.

"You got to agree with me," he said, his voice trembling with the remnants of his anger. "It's a trap. A no good, lousy trap."

Kitty sighed. Her lips felt dry and ragged; her sinuses were stuffed and made her head throb with congestion and fever.

"Well, if it's a trap," she said, wringing the sponge into the new, gleaming sink, "why the hell don't you do something?"

"What?" His strong fingers spread to the air like he wanted to grab a throat and choke it. "What can I do, Kitty?"

She wiped her fingers on a crisp dish towel and untied the apron and hung it on the handle of the refrigerator door. They had been playing the same scene for six months. Ever since he bought the house.

"Do anything you want to do," she said, touching the small of her back, where a new, peculiar pain spiralled. "Is that clear, Fred? Anything you want."

He moved ahead of her and bent to pick up the small therens.

Sometimes she liked to watch the way he moved. It reminded her of their old days together. When he had felt free and each day of their future was a new, bright surprise. The gift of his love, then, had been like a Christmas present. Now, it was nothing but a worn out toy. It lay neglected in one corner of their lives, hidden by the need of money, by the creeping boredom of his routine job.

"I wish I had something to tell you," she said, kneeling beside him. "I really wish I did."

Side by side, crouched at the table leg, they looked at each other. Kitty reached a hand to touch his cheek. It felt warm and his dark eyes seemed puzzled by her sudden burst of tenderness.

"What a beautiful way to spend a Saturday night," she laughed softly, recalling other Saturday nights … in parked cars, in top rows of movie houses.

Impulsively, she leaned in and kissed him full on the mouth. They hadn't kissed like this for weeks. Or was it months?

"No excuses tonight," she whispered. "Even if I have a fever of a hundred and ten."

She put her arms around his neck and drew him in close. If she could recall the fervor of their love, maybe she could recall some spark of his ambition, too. That knack he had once of shucking off things that bothered him, as a dog nonchalantly shakes off rain.

"Are you nuts?" he said. "They'll be here in half an hour."

"Half an hour's enough," she answered, smiling. "I'd rather have a nickel now than five dollars later …."

She watched her insinuation soften the harshness that had darkened his face only moments before. Maybe, in some way, she had helped to cause his deep unhappiness. If so, she would do what she could to help cure it, too.

"I love you," she murmured.

She closed her eyes and tilted her mouth to his.

"You're a good girl," he said. "I'm sorry I …."

She ended his words abruptly, pressing her tongue into his mouth and squeezing her hunched up body into his lap. Some bread crumbs pressed into her knees, reminding her again that she hadn't been much of a housekeeper for him.

"I'll be good for you," she said. "We're going to have fun again, Fred. You'll see."

Enthusiasm stirred, warming her with hopes and with deep intentions.

"And something else," she murmured against his neck. "I'm going to get a job, Fred. Go back to work and help out, so that all the burden won't be on you."

His fingers were already probing beneath the buttons of her blouse. She felt his eagerness and realized how starved he must be. For love. For physicality. For companionship. She put her hand over his fingers and moved them down onto her breast.

"Take me," she whispered. "Use me, darling."

She stared up at the underside of the table, her gaze moving at random across the raw wood grain. She felt cozy in this odd place. Like making love under a boardwalk. The hurried, hidden quality of it made Kitty forget for the moment that she was married ... that she had a perfect right to this.

She leaned against the molding and spread her legs, feeling the dress pull tight across her knees.

"This is ridiculous," he said. "Let's go where it's comfortable."

"What for?" she laughed.

"For your sake," he muttered, his words breathless now.

"Don't worry about me. I'm adaptable."

"You're crazy, you mean."

But she heard the touch of laughter in his voice and knew that it tickled him, too, this silliness that challenged their dreary routine.

"Go on," she said. "Pull my...."

He kissed her again, but harder this time, pressing her blonde head lightly back against the wall. She felt the sudden surge in him that told her he didn't need directions. His palm moved from her breast downward, cupping hard against her. No preliminaries. No dalliance. She felt how he had to have her quickly. He had gotten into the urgent mood, making passion a challenge, an agile goal that could leap away if not grabbed immediately.

Kitty smiled to herself and raised her hips, making room for his touch. His body told her that it had ceased to be a game. The heat of him melted her random thoughts into simple desire.

She slid along the linoleum, helping his fingers unfasten her stockings and pull at her underthings till she lay free and accessible.

"Go ahead," she whispered.

He came to her.

A small cry escaped her lips as she felt the surge of him. One knee knocked the table leg as she moved to encircle him. How strange it felt, the hard floor bruising her spine and banging her elbows. Uncomfortable, really ... and ridiculous too, just as Fred had warned.

Yet through it all, she felt the soft resilience of silken pillows beneath her and she knew in her heart that she had latched onto a precious secret.

"Good?" he rasped, moving with her.

She caught him by the shoulders and braced herself, steadying for the final move that would both imprison and free her. Her stomach knotted like a child's fist and she caught her lower lip between her teeth, swinging high on an arc of taut, elastic nerves.

His own gasp, a familiar, controlled sound, told Kitty that it was happening for them both. That at last they were sharing again what Fate had meant for them to share.

She rode out giant waves, feeling them ebb gradually into small ripples of pleasure. And finally she lay exhausted, her sweaty cheek against his cheek.

"Are you all right?" he said.

Kitty wet her lips with the point of her tongue. "You know something, Fred?"

"What?"

Kitty ran her fingertips lightly through the deep widow's peak of his dark hair. "I'm glad I married you."

The feeling stayed with her while they dressed—making themselves presentable for the arrival of Rose and Mark. Their rambling suburban home glowed with soft lights filtering through orange colored lamp shades. It was a comfortable place to live, Kitty thought as she set out boxes of candy and a bowl of fruit. Not yet too cluttered with possessions, there was still an air of freshness and brightness about the rooms. Optimism … that's what the atmosphere hummed with. Or was it simply her own optimism that had been suddenly reborn?

Kitty moved quickly, punching up sofa pillows, opening a window here and there to let in the Apirl evening. She felt ten years younger and alive with a new tempo. No more creeping despair. No more bills piling higher than Fred's income. She grinned to herself, as though for the moment her feelings must remain a secret.

The triple tone doorbell rang and she let Fred go to answer. She smiled at his hulking, football player walk, so civilized inside a dark blue suit with narrow lapels. The desk job he held had faded his naturally dark complexion. She knew he didn't belong inside. He needed weather on his face, the outdoors to move around in. And she wished, suddenly, that Fred had finished college instead of quitting everything just because they had gotten married.

"Rose, you're looking beautiful. … Hi, Mark, old man."

Kitty listened to the greetings and moved in to kiss her sister and her brother-in-law. Happiness was Rose's speciality, Kitty had always thought. It glistened softly in her gray eyes and smoothed out the wrinkles that at thirty-five had begun to change the meaning of the laugh lines around her mouth.

They embraced and Kitty slipped off Rose's mink stole, carrying it with delicate care to the closet.

"You're looking marvelous," Kitty said over her shoulder. "How're the children?"

"They don't like military school, that's certain," Rose said. "I think we'll probably be bringing them home after Mark and I get back from Paris next month."

"Mark is smart. He knows how to take vacations," Kitty said, unable to keep a tinge of envy from her tone.

"It's part of his job," Rose answered matter-of-factly.

"Well, I wish it were part of Fred's job, too."

Kitty shut the closet door and glanced past her sister's flowered dress to where Mark was sipping the highball Fred had given him. He was shorter than Fred and quite slender. Shrewdness sparkled from him like gold leaf. One could see it in the relaxation of his shoulders and the neat line of his body tapering down to the expensive brogues. As he tasted the drink, enjoyment spread across his face. He was close to forty, yet his capacity to enjoy things made him look twenty-five. No strain or frustration was evident in his face.

Fred, in comparison, looked tired. Stronger, but worn out. He needed something, Kitty thought, but she couldn't exactly define what.

"You have a lovely home," Rose said.

"Oh, this is your first time here, isn't it?" Kitty said, making conversation. "In the rush of things, I'd almost forgotten. Come, let me show you around."

"How about your drinks?" Mark called after them.

"Yes," Kitty said absently. "Let's all take our drinks and look at the place together."

Mark gave her a glass, smiling down at her the way only Mark could smile … a protective covering for his little sister-in-law, something to keep her dry in the rain, sheltered from the wind. Kitty thought his face must be his fortune. It radiated the kind of love every woman dreamed of. No wonder he was chief regional salesman for Knit Spun Dresses. He could melt any woman with that smile.

They toured the house from the finished basement to the semi-finished attic and Kitty gave them the spiel that went with it. She remembered how proud she had once felt, going through the various rooms. But with the passing of the weeks, the house seemed to shrink, going from a spectacle to normalcy and then to dullness. Now, as she led her relatives around, she tried to show them, not the house, but the spark of hope that had burned bright only moments before. Soon, she intended to make new curtains. Soon. she would buy pictures for the walls, do over the bathroom with ceramic tile.

But even as she spoke, Kitty knew she was merely mouthing words.

"It's lovely," she heard Rose saying.

But how could this place possibly impress Rose when her own home, sprawling on two acres of Long Island lawn, was twice the size and kept spotless by two maids?

Whatever Kitty might dream of, she knew there would always be someone who had more. She sneezed suddenly and Fred pressed a Kleenex into her hand. Feeling weak, she leaned against him for a moment and hung onto his sleeve, wanting him somehow to reassure her.

"You ought to be in bed with that," Rose said gently.

Kitty shook her head and smiled through her burning eyelids. "I'm all right," she said. "Really I am."

"Let's go back to the living room and sit down," Mark suggested in the deep voice that always reminded Kitty of an old time radio commentator.

Fred put his arm around her waist. She could feel its thick muscle guiding her and she wanted to tell him not to worry.

"It's only a little cold," she said, smiling self-consciously. "I wish everybody wouldn't make such a fuss."

As though to prove that she really felt fine, she tilted her drink and swallowed it down, indicating that she was out to have a good time.

But as she sat down on the sofa, she felt her head beginning to spin and her legs going weak. She patted Fred's hand and shrugged, pretending that her complaint a moment before had been a false alarm.

She saw him believing her and his attention turning to other matters.

"I guess this is going to come as a surprise to everyone," Fred began, "including my wife. But I'm giving notice right now that this place is up for rent. So, Rose, if you hear of anyone who's looking, you'll tell 'em to give us a buzz, all right?"

In the moment of shocked pause that followed, Fred poured Kitty another drink. His dark, gleaming eyes seemed filled with a new radiance. They reflected the optimism she had been feeling a brief time before, as though hope had drained from her veins and travelled along into his.

Then she remembered. *Do something. Do anything you want....* These had been her words.

Fred was only taking her up on what she had said. He had chosen this way to meet the challenge of their money tangles.

Kitty swallowed her second drink, realizing that she had no choice but to go along with him. Be a good sport.

"That's right," she nodded, telling Rose and Mark with her nonchalance that they could believe Fred. "This place is big enough for a family with two kids. The school is only three blocks north and shopping's convenient. Keep it in mind for us, will you?"

She looked from one to the other of them, daring either of them to show pity.

Rose said, "Of course," at the same time making a strenuous effort to cover her puzzlement by examining a fresh chip off her nail polish.

Mark opened his cigarette case and offered it around. "Swimming is so close by, too," he said easily. "You'll get someone before the summer's in."

Fred stretched out his legs and opened his jacket. "I'll give anybody who wants the place a two year lease," he said. "Kitty and I are moving up."

Kitty shut off the sound of his voice and settled into her own gloom. She dared not glance at either Rose or Mark, knowing she could not cope with the expressions she found there. Instead, she let Fred fix her another drink and nursed it along, hating Fred, hating herself. At the moment, hating even Mark and Rose.

Later, when they had gone, she turned abruptly from Fred and went into the bedroom to undress. She heard him follow, felt the touch of his warm hand on her arm.

Angrily, she spun on him. "Why did you spring it on me like that?" she spat. "You shocked all of us half to death. And you ruined the evening!"

Fred merely smiled, undaunted by her rage. He hung his jacket in the closet and pulled loose his tie. "I'm sorry about that. But I thought if I didn't say it right out...you know, commit myself in front of others...you wouldn't take me seriously. Or that you would try to argue me out of it."

Kitty felt her throat beginning to tighten. A fever had started to throb and her brain felt all fuzzed over. "I don't know what to say," her words were hoarse. "It sounds so absurd, that's all. Moving out of a house we own hardly a year. What got into you, Fred? What are you thinking?"

"You know very well what I'm thinking," he said. "To save money. We'll rent the place and that'll more than take care of the mortgage. As for you and me, two rooms is enough for us for the time being. I'm going to quit my job, too, you see. Start all over."

She stared at him for a moment. Then she slipped out of her high heels and bent to massage one arch. "Sounds pretty drastic."

"It is drastic."

"You sound so proud of yourself," Kitty said flatly.

"Well, I am," Fred answered, rolling up his shirt sleeves. "Besides, it was your idea in a way. To feel young again."

She caught the twinkle in Fred's eye reminding her of what had occurred in the kitchen. A tight knot of nausea choked in her throat. "I guess I was feeling inspired," she sighed. "But I didn't honestly think for a minute it was going to lead to this."

The future seemed hidden behind a mist rolling damply to smother her. What could she say to Fred, now that he felt so sure of himself?

She padded across to the bed and snuggled down beneath the quilt's comforting warmth. Maybe, in the morning when her head felt clearer, they would have a good talk. Spell out the details, plan a line of action. That was how her father had worked, with precision. She must make Fred see that they could not give up everything they had achieved. They must start from where they were and build up ....

Fred climbed in beside her. He propped the pillow behind his head and sat smoking a final cigarette.

"You know what I'm going to do?" he said musingly.

"What?" Kitty spoke into the pillow, only half hearing him.

"Enjoy myself. Have a little fun for a change. Wouldn't you like that, Kitty? To get rid of all these stupid responsibilities and live like the birds?"

She had heard it so often. And what did it mean? "Birds have wings," she said bitterly.

Fred laughed softly. "So they have. But we have brains, Kitty. At least, I hope so."

"Yes," Kitty murmured, already half asleep. She didn't have the strength to tell him what she felt. How fervently she hoped that they really did have brains enough not to give up their very roots.

CHAPTER TWO

By morning, Kitty felt that she must have dreamed the whole thing. She awoke in the same familiar bed and smelled the same familiar odor of coffee and toast that she smelled every Sunday when Fred got up first and made breakfast.

The congestion in her head had subsided. She put on the white corduroy bathrobe that Rose had sent her for a birthday present and went to find Fred, to touch him, to assure herself of the reality and the security that had felt so slippery in her dreams.

He stood naked to the waist, pouring orange juice into squat glasses.

"Feel better this morning?" he said with a sprightly tone.

"Much." Kitty sat down at the table and unfolded a napkin. "Know what I'd like to do today?"

"What?"

"Go to an auction," she said. "I was thinking about the study. I think it needs a rug in front of the bookcase."

"It's good enough as it is," Fred answered, unplugging the electric coffee maker and balancing it on a trivet beside the salt shaker.

"But you like rugs."

"Whoever rents the place might not like rugs."

Kitty drank her juice slowly. The flavor of late spring oranges went sour on her tongue. "Then you did mean it," she said after a moment.

"Of course. I meant every word," Fred said evenly. "Every damned word and let's not forget it."

"Well, you don't have to lose your temper."

Anger exploded from her, as though a stranger had pulled a favorite toy from her grasp.

"Then stop asking me the same thing over and over," Fred said harshly. "I told you last night, Kitty. We're going to break out of this rat race."

He was breathing hard and the thick muscles of his chest heaved. Kitty wondered why it didn't frighten her to see him this way. He could crush her, break her in half before he even thought about it. Yet she felt somehow withdrawn from him, as though their lives ran in separate directions.

"Do whatever you want," Kitty said, buttering a slice of light toast and watching the melting grease ooze into the air holes. "But make it sensible. If you think I'm just going to walk out of here with my toothbrush in a knapsack, you're mistaken. I mean, it's silly, Fred, can't you see that? How much better off could we be, holed up in a cheap furnished room somewhere? That's what we moved out of. Or don't you remember?"

Fred came to the table and dropped some more bread into the toaster. "I remember. And you know something? I remember that we were happier in that furnished room than we've ever been since."

"The grass is always greener ...."

"Maybe. But I'm going to try, Kitty. I can't go on like this. I hate working in that foolish jewelry store. Do you know what I do all day? Exercise my finger dialling telephone numbers. People who can't pay their bills are all I ever speak to. It's getting me down, Kitty. I seem to have lost touch with everything that's fun."

Kitty tasted her coffee black. "It's all in the mind," she said. "If you're not happy here, you won't be happy anywhere."

"What are you trying to tell me?" he said quietly. "That you won't cooperate?"

"Lower your voice," she said to his lowered tone. "The neighbors will hear you."

"The hell with the neighbors," he screamed. "This is important."

"Well," Kitty said evenly, "I have a few plans of my own, if you want to hear them. Now sit down and stop making such a ruckus."

She pushed a chair out for him and waited till he was sitting. Then she poured him a cup of coffee and added the right amount of sugar and milk.

"What I'm going to do," she said, pushing the cup in front of him, "is get a job and help you out."

"It's about time."

"You don't sound appreciative."

"Tell me about this job of yours."

His sharp, demanding eyes and his dark stubble of beard made him prickly as a porcupine to look at and Kitty gazed away from him to the faded yellow curtains fluttering in the morning sunlight. "I'm still pretty good with my shorthand," she said. "I could bring in a hundred dollars a week, couldn't I?"

"That's what you think."

"Well, seventy five, anyway. And that's most of the mortgage. You could quit your job and work part time. Maybe go back to school, Fred. Would you like that?"

"Of course I'd like that," Fred answered. "But you're dreaming. Even if I could get a part-time job, it would take me years to finish school at night."

"And you don't want to depend on me, is that it?"

Fred shrugged. "You might get pregnant."

"You're evading."

"Well, who the hell wants to live on a woman's money? It gives me the creeps just to think about it."

Kitty smiled. There was something naïve about Fred that she enjoyed. No matter what happened, she would always know what he was thinking. It showed all over his face like jam.

"All right, we'll compromise," she said. "We'll work alternate years and you can go to school during the day."

"But it comes out to the same time," he said. "Can't you see?"

"You just want your own way."

"And you just want yours."

Kitty grinned. To fight with Fred was like fighting with the wind. You never knew which way it might blow next. She leaned over and kissed his rough chin. What difference did it make, after all, where they lived, as long as they were together?

"All right," she said. "We'll rent out the house. But don't go blaming me if you begin to feel trapped again."

Fred munched his toast. "That was too easy," he said. "What are you really thinking?"

Kitty yawned. "I'm not thinking anything," she said. "I just feel good. You make me feel good."

"That means I'm sounding pretty stupid this morning," Fred said warily.

"Don't be difficult. I love you. Take it for granted that whatever you want, no matter how stupid it is, you'll have it, if I can get it for you."

Fred poured more coffee into her cup.

She ran her fingers along the fuzz on his arms. "Come on, baby," she teased. "Smile."

After breakfast, Kitty put the dishes into the automatic washer, turned the various shiny knobs and forgot about domestic matters for the time being. She had been thinking about the rug somewhere deep in her brain, and now it seemed engraved there, vivid and necessary as breath.

She dressed, gazing out the window at a bright sky that looked both mild and kind. Why not go into New York? She hadn't been to the city for weeks and she felt a sudden need for company, for the push and crush of people.

Fred came into the bedroom carrying the papers that had been delivered to the doorstep and flopped down on his belly, pulling out the employment section and folding it back to the female help wanted.

"You're gonna be a secretary?" he said.

"I thought I might like something in import-export," she said. "Maybe get a chance to use some of my Spanish."

"Okay, let's see what's available."

She heard him rattling pages while she dressed, smoothing the line of her stockings and noticing in the narrow door mirror a slight puffiness around the ankles. Otherwise, she looked pretty well today. Her blonde hair sat in a neat tuck of waves that cupped her head and the two high spots of color on her cheeks made her eyes glisten. When she tilted her head sideways, she reminded herself of Rose, except that Rose had a certain calmness that was missing from her own taut flesh.

"Want to work down at the Brooklyn docks?"

Fred's voice kidded her. She had known from the beginning that he would not take her seriously, yet she couldn't resist her right to try.

"Can't you find anything further away?" she bantered back.

"Wait, I'm looking."

Boyishly, he bounced his legs as he read and she watched the tight line of his hips beneath the striped pajamas. He was a basic type. A meat and potatoes man. You had to treat them with patience and lots of love. Fred was the kind who repaid such feelings with an avid loyalty.

"Here's something even better," he said. "That's if you know German and French."

"How about Greek?"

He let the paper fall to the floor and turned to look at her. "Say, what are you doing, anyhow?"

"Getting dressed."

"Yeah, I can see that for myself."

"Good for you, dear. You're getting alert."

Fred sat up, scratching his head lazily and following her motions, half with curiosity and half with irritation.

"No church," he said. "I'm not going to church."

"Fine."

She spun quickly, taking a last full glance at herself and feeling satisfied that she looked good enough to be taken seriously at an auction.

"Well, so long," she said, transferring the change purse and other small objects from her brown purse to her black one.

"Where are you going?" Fred demanded.

"To the city," she said casually. "I told you before."

"You didn't tell me anything."

"Yes I did. I'm going to the rug auction, remember?"

A low groan told Kitty that she had connected with home plate. "I thought we finished with that," he said.

"With what, dear?"

"With spending money needlessly."

"But it isn't needless. It's necessary."

"A rug is necessary?"

"A rug for that room is necessary, yes."

"Oh, Kitty, please." His face contorting with the pain of lost patience, Fred got up and came to her. "Please don't spoil a nice Sunday with your need to keep up with the Joneses," he said, gripping her arms and holding her steady. "Try, just for once, to be sensible, will you?"

"I'm being sensible," she protested. "How can you rent a house if it looks like a barn?"

"It doesn't look like a .... Oh, for chrissake!"

Together, they felt it happening between them again. That wall of concrete that neither one could get through to reach the other.

"Please let go of my arms, Fred. You're hurting me."

"Aren't you at least going to try?" he said dismally.

"Try what?"

"To understand."

"I do understand."

"If you understood anything, we wouldn't have gotten into this predicament in the first place. We'd have bought a house we could afford instead of trying to rival Rose. Or maybe we'd have rented another apartment, who knows? But you've got to come to your senses, honey. No rugs. No new car this year. Rock bottom, do you understand me? A little austerity now so that we can get back on our feet before we're too old to enjoy it."

Kitty heard the words, but she knew that Fred was only kidding himself. "We lived tight for a long time," she said coldly. "And where did it get us? It was you who wanted this place. You said it would be like money in the bank."

"Yes, I know, I know." Fred shook his head with exasperation. "But all that's changed. I've given up trying to find out how to do things the easy way. We've got to buckle down, Kitty. And right now."

"All right, darling," she said, patting his shoulder. "But a little rug for twenty-five dollars isn't going to make or break us now."

She watched him walk to the open window and take in a deep breath as though someone had clamped a vise around his throat.

"Kitty," he said without turning to face her, "no rugs!"

Kitty took a comb from her dressing table and ran it slowly through her hair. He was in that kind of a mood. A dray horse with blinders. When he was like this, she couldn't budge him and she knew she had better not try.

"All right, darling," she said brightly. "Whatever you say. But can't we at least go and see how an auction works? I've never been to one and it is Sunday."

CHAPTER THREE

The one characteristic about Fred that annoyed Kitty to the very marrow was his stubbornness. She felt that she always had to work at making him realize that he wasn't the only one in the house entitled to consideration.

And it was the fear of becoming invisible, of getting trampled underfoot, that had made her hold out for going to New York. If he hadn't wanted to come along, that was his business.

She sat alone in the convertible, feeling the wind lap the scarf tied around her neck and feeling disappointed that Fred had not given in, just this once.

She parked the car in a garage and made a pact with herself that she would have a good time today without him. She would take herself out and forget her troubles ... and Fred, too.

Unaccustomed to the crowds, she watched people milling around her like mechanical toys gone haywire. What was the matter with Fred, anyway, that he wanted to give up the house in the country, with its precious bit of greenery, for all this cement and soot and noise?

The more she thought about Fred, the angrier Kitty boiled. And the more she boiled, the more she refused to believe that they couldn't have found another way out of their problems.

She strolled past Radio City, but the thought of sitting through a whole show by herself felt gruesome and she crossed over to Whelan's. She phoned Rose, hoping to arrange a last minute coffee klatch with her sister.

"Hello, Mark? Yes, I'm much better, thank you ...."

Mark, who understood and liked people, didn't take long to discover that she had stranded herself alone in the middle of the city. When she had hung up and gone into Schrafft's for a sandwich to pass the time till they came to get her, Kitty felt satisfied that Fred, by comparison, was a selfish boor who didn't care at all what she felt or what happened to her.

The sore throat that had gone away during the night began to return and Kitty admitted to herself that she should have put up the top on the car.

Yet the more she considered Fred's position if she should get stuck in bed for a week, the better she felt about it. Snuggled into a corner booth of the restaurant, Kitty drank cups of tea with lemon and nibbled at a sandwich, figuring in her mind all the money he would be spending on doctors and medicine. Much more, no doubt, than the cost of a small rug.

By the time Mark arrived, she felt almost happy, her insides warm with food and her pulse vivid with expectation.

"Where's Rose?" she asked Mark.

"She couldn't make it," Mark answered easily. "There were a couple of packages to send off to the boys at school and I thought I'd just come by and get you while she was wrapping them. Say, that looks good."

"Sliced chicken. Have some."

"Think I will."

Mark took off his hat and swung it onto a hook, making himself comfortable on the seat opposite her.

"You know," Mark said, folding his white hands on the polished table top, "we've never gotten to know each other well, have we?"

He said it like a simple fact and Kitty did not feel pressed to reply.

"I like Schrafft's brand of tea," she said. "I wonder why they've never sold it in retail stores."

"Rose is always saying to me that we ought to go visit Kitty and Fred. Or that we should have you over. That's true, Kitty. You and Fred should come visit us more often. Family's an important thing in life."

"Yes," Kitty said flatly. She resisted the sudden urge to tell Mark that Fred didn't feel like family at all. He seemed more like a stranger. Cold, indifferent, selfish. But she was in no mood for unpleasantness. It wouldn't seem quite polite, somehow, to spoil Mark's decency with her own troubles.

"I'll have another pot of tea," Kitty said when the waitress had taken Mark's order. "And one of those curly chocolate things I saw you carrying by."

"The Vienna truffles?"

"Is that what they are?"

When the waitress left, Kitty leaned back against the wooden partition and, from her safe distance, smiled warmly at Mark.

This was the first Sunday in months that she had gone someplace without Fred. Now, with Mark to take care of things, she relaxed and gave herself to the delicious glow of freedom spreading through her insides. She had been like a bird in a cage. Now she had sprung the lock and flown free.

"It's not often I get into the city," Kitty said, dawdling over her cup. "I think I feel something like a tourist today." She smiled at Mark, a pleasant, sisterly smile, and felt glad for Rose's good fortune.

She saw in the light of Mark's steady eyes behind his glasses that he had picked up her meaning.

"Would you like to stroll for a while before we drive back? I didn't tell Rose what time to expect us."

"Yes, I would," she answered frankly. "It gets lonesome out in the country. And a bit repetitious from one day to the next."

Mark nodded with understanding. He steered her out of the restaurant and into the flurry of human traffic.

Now Kitty did not feel dizzy from all the confusion, but exhilarated. She looked forward to a good time like a toy that she would soon clutch in happy surprise.

"I want to apologize," she said, keeping step with Mark, "for all the strangeness last night."

"About the house, you mean?"

"Yes .... That and other things. You must have sensed how edgy Fred was."

"I didn't notice anything of the sort."

She felt that Mark was being kind. That, in his gentlemanly fashion, he would dull the pain of her embarrassment. She decided that she would not mention Fred again. That she would simply let things happen as they would and make the most of the hours.

"You know," she said, "I came into the city today to go to a furniture auction, but I lost my nerve at the last minute."

It seemed to Kitty, as she heard the words coming from herself, that what she said was true. If she had the money, she would have the nerve. But without money, how could she have dared to look at all those pretty things and watched them moving into everyone's hands but her own?

"Would you like to find your nerve again?" Mark smiled, not chiding her for being foolish, but merely asking.

Impulsively, Kitty nodded. "But don't you think we ought to call Rose first? She might wonder .... "

"I doubt it," Mark grinned. "You know how she likes to fuss about making fancy dinners. She'll be glad for the extra hour before we arrive."

"Fine," Kitty said, taking out her compact as they walked and checking the make-up around her nose. The one thing that gave her confidence was the feeling that she looked perfect. Something in Mark's manner told her that she looked beautiful. For her own satisfaction, she had to see it for herself. She smiled at her reflection, knowing that she looked better than usual today ... even if Fred hadn't noticed.

They rode across to the West Side in a cab.

"Is this the building?" Kitty said, a trifle disappointed at the bleakness and the shabby atmosphere.

"You never know what you'll find inside," Mark said.

Since it had been her idea, Kitty stopped protesting and followed obediently beside him.

They entered a large, crowded room that smelled of dust and sweat. Dimly lit, the high ceilinged room felt more like a warehouse with pieces of odd furniture standing around in shadow, like ghosts waiting to be called up.

The auctioneer's voice, loud, insistent, seemed to goad the audience. The people that Kitty saw looked crude and grimy. She drew herself into a small knot, trying to keep from the touch of them. This was certainly not what she had imagined ... not like any auction she had seen in the movies.

"Did you have anything special in mind?" Mark asked, holding her arm and bending himself around her in a way that seemed to fend off the approach of strangers.

"A rug," Kitty said. "But it's probably been sold by now."

"Well, let's go up and see."

He started to move her through the crowd.

"And even if it hasn't," Kitty said protestingly, "I probably won't like it anyway."

"Why, Kitty Miner," Mark whispered into her ear. "I didn't know you were a snob."

Startled, she stared up into his laughing eyes. She had never seen Mark like this before. Devilish, playfully debonair. He seemed somehow years younger than Rose and Kitty stiffened at the awareness.

Without answering, Kitty moved among the random assortment, feeling glad that she had an excuse to busy herself with something. She was not looking at Mark, but the sense of his presence beside her made Kitty awkward and self conscious in a new and strange flush of warmth.

"The rugs are behind that credenza," Mark said.

His voice indicated nothing, as though the moment between them had never happened ... as though a bolt of summer lightning had flashed across the sky, leaving a vast, very ordinary calmness.

"Oh, yes," she murmured. "I see."

Kitty moved around the dusty furniture to where a dozen carpets lay rolled and piled into a pyramid.

"Well, what can I tell about them like this?" she said. "The least they could do is roll them open for display."

"I guess it's finders, keepers," Mark said. "It's not like the Parke Bernet Galleries, after all. But then again, neither are the bids."

"You've been to the Parke Bernet?" she said, knowing that of course he had. Mark could afford to go there. Rose's home was furnished with a perfect taste.

"Did you notice in the papers," he said for an answer, "whether or not there's something on there today?"

"No. I didn't look."

She said it bravely, yet she felt Mark catching her in the bare-faced lie.

He caught it and examined it and thrust it aside as though it had been a mere game on Kitty's part.

"Well, we can go now," he said lightly, "and see for ourselves."

"Oh, no," Kitty blurted.

"Why not?" Mark persisted calmly.

"I just. ... I guess I'm not really in the mood."

How could she tell him? She took out her compact again and patted the curve of her nose with a small powder puff, hiding the devil in her heart which struggled to take advantage of Mark. If they went, she knew that he would buy something for her. Innocently, of course. Yet she dared not accept presents ... not even a small rug. It would be like a slap in the face to Fred and she didn't want to hit him quite that hard.

"Let's just wait and see about that little one over there," Kitty said blindly, nodding at the rug at the bottom of the pile. She needed time to collect her senses, to come back to her own depth.

"All right," Mark said. "Whatever you wish."

"I really had my heart set on just looking today."

"Did you?"

Again, a gleam like the wicked stab of a dagger glinted in his eyes and was gone.

"Well, why should I want to buy anything?" Kitty shrugged. "We're moving out soon anyway. It wouldn't be sensible."

"No, of course it wouldn't," he said gravely.

Kitty felt that in his own subtle way, Mark was enjoying her stories. Maybe Rose, because she was the direct and sincere type, never flirted with him.

Quickly, she turned off the thoughts and conjectures beginning to spin through her mind.

"Maybe we'd better go," she said in a low voice. "I think I'm just wasting our time." Insecurity trembled in her tone. She felt startled by the quick turn of events in her imagination and anxious that Mark should not discover them.

"And your rug?"

"It was only a whim." She sighed. "I'd really rather go back and help Rose make dinner."

"No you wouldn't, Kitty, so why pretend? Let's just wait and see what we can find here and maybe you'll be pleasantly surprised after all."

Mark's honesty trapped her and she felt speechless.

"All right?" he said, squeezing her arm.

Kitty nodded. She wanted to run … away from Mark and from her own impulsive nonsense. She had no business here in the first place. No business doing anything without Fred's permission.

Yet if she made a move to leave so abruptly, she would have to explain. And Mark would see through whatever she might try to say. Better to stay and wait it out than to embarrass herself.

The big room, smoky and airless, seemed to close in around her. What had she been thinking of to let Mark bring her here in the first place? It was a mistake, but one that she could not readily correct.

The auctioneer's voice droned on, wheedling, soothing, urging, spinning its tales snakelike. It seemed an eternity before the rugs would come up. Perspiration began to gather on her upper lip, making her itch nervously.

Mark took out his cigarette case, but she did not take one. Suddenly she knew that she dared not take anything from him ... not even something so innocent as a cigarette.

"How are the boys?" she said to fill in the lull between them and needing also the comfort of remembered domesticity.

"Restless," Mark said. "Straining to get home. I don't know what Rose wants to do with them once they are home, though. With all the travelling we have to do, it'll be tough."

Kitty couldn't imagine anything being tough for Mark. His competent mouth knew how to smile so steadily. She sighed and tried to think of other subjects for conversation.

"... And now ladies and gentlemen, four Sarouks of the finest ..."

Mark nudged her. "Here come your carpets," he said.

"Oh, good," Kitty answered without enthusiasm. She had been standing too long and the soles of her feet burned. Suddenly, she could not have cared less about the rugs.

"Look, he's putting your little one up first."

Kitty looked. The worn out red and blue design seemed to reflect her own feelings. Some time ago, she had ceased to sparkle. Now she felt limp, tired, in need of a place to sit down and refresh herself.

"... What am I offered? ..."

From behind them a male voice said, "Fifteen."

A pause.

The auctioneer leaned forward. "Fifteen dollars for this genuine, hand made..."

Another voice said, "Twenty."

"Ladies and gentlemen...twenty dollars, twenty dollars, twenty...."

"Twenty-five."

Kitty heard the explosion of sound and realized that it was Mark's voice. Horrified, she stood quite still, choked with shame, but unable to protest audibly.

"...twenty-five, twenty-five..."

"Thirty," called the first deep voice that had started the bidding.

"...thirty, thirty. Is this beautiful piece?..."

"Thirty-five," Mark said.

"Thirty-five...thirty-five. Gentlemen, thirty-five. What am I offered? Thirty-five.... Thirty-five. Going once, going..."

"It's yours," Mark said, squeezing her arm. "Now, how are you going to get the darned thing home?"

Numbly, Kitty followed him to where the rug lay. Already her mind leaped ahead to the scene with Fred. He wouldn't understand it. She didn't understand it herself.

"Now, this is a very lovely piece," Mark said with enthusiasm. "I hope it will give you a great deal of pleasure."

CHAPTER FOUR

Kitty trembled.

"But I promised Rose you'd come back for dinner. She's expecting you."

Kitty stood beside Mark's car as he leaned with one elbow resting on her new rug, poked out the side window. She wanted to get in and go with him. In fact, she wanted to ride to the ends of the earth, where Fred would never find her and she wouldn't have to try to explain.

"Well, I ought to call my husband," she said shakily, "and tell him I'll be late. He doesn't know when to expect me home and I didn't leave any supper for him."

"Then why don't you invite him along?"

The innocent question bounced off Kitty's head like a ping pong ball. She knew that Fred would make a scene about the rug and that he wouldn't care who was around at the time.

"I think he caught my cold," Kitty said evasively. "He wasn't even dressed when I left the house this morning. I don't think it would be good for him to come out this evening. The weather's been so changeable."

It was simply a formal excuse in order to be courteous and she said it because she knew that Mark would understand.

Pleadingly, yet almost brazenly, she looked up into his face, trusting him not to make objection.

For answer, Mark fished in his pocket. "Here's some change," he said. "You phone and straighten things out the way you want them, Kitty. I'll wait for you here in the car."

Kitty smiled, feeling warmly secure again. He was such a sweet man, Mark.

She bounced off to the pay phone and called home, preparing herself with clenched jaw for Fred's nastiness.

And when she told him about the afternoon, how nice Mark had been to her and the unexpected present she was bringing home, the nastiness that she had bargained for broke loose.

Kitty held the receiver away from her ear as the words poured out, sharp and hurtful, burning her with indignation as sleet would burn her cheeks.

"... And you'd better come home right now, Kitty. I said right now."

Kitty wet her lips. "For your kind of attention," she said, "I don't have to hurry home. You'll see me when I get there." And quite gently, she lowered the receiver, glad that she could be a lady even if Fred had no qualms about forgetting his manners.

"All arranged," Kitty said brightly to Mark as she came out, pulling her gloves on again and dancing along as though Fred had rolled out a red carpet to her every wish.

"Good," Mark said, leaning across to open the door for her, then slamming it shut again, his arm grazing her lap as he did so.

Kitty stayed with Mark and Rose as late as she decently could without upsetting Rose's schedule for the next day.

And when she had retrieved the convertible from the garage, she drove toward home slowly, hoping that Fred had burned himself out by now and would be sleeping.

She turned into their block and peered down the street, only to see that the lights were burning in the living room window. He hadn't gone to sleep at all. He had probably been sitting there gathering fuel for the flame.

Well, whatever he might say Kitty felt that she had a ready answer and her fingers tightened on the steering wheel as she churned up the army of her defenses.

Quickly, she pulled into the garage and lowered the door and snapped the lock over. It had been such a good day, really. And such a congenial evening. By contrast, the fighting with Fred seemed so cheap, so futile.

She pushed open the front door and stepped inside to the sweet, heavy scent of his pipe and the heavy, sour odor of burned lamb chops.

"It's like a cave in here," Kitty said, setting her purse and gloves on a side table beneath the foyer mirror. In the lamp light she studied the lines around her nose and the deepening lines on her forehead that mapped out her daily tensions. She felt, suddenly, that living with Fred was making her grow old before her time. If she had had any sense, she wouldn't have rushed into their marriage....

"I take it you enjoyed yourself," came Fred's voice, brittle and poised.

"I did," Kitty answered, still watching herself in the mirror. She was recalling the fun days back in high school, with dates every weekend and nothing more to worry her than cheerleading practice and her marks in intermediate algebra. She frowned and touched one pencilled eyebrow with a fingernail. Those days seemed so far off that they might have belonged to another woman. "I had a very good time altogether," she said crisply. "And Rose and Mark missed you."

"I'm sure."

"Well, they did," Kitty replied. She didn't like to talk from one room to another and yet she couldn't help but postpone facing him and the scowling face that would inevitably mar her lovely day.

"But you?" his voice insinuated. "You didn't miss me. You're sure of that, too, aren't you?"

Kitty went into the living room. He had changed from his pajamas to a pair of loose corduroy slacks and he looked so homey, so relaxed that she wanted to cry at the thought of them moving back to a furnished room.

"Of course I missed you," she said, leaning over and kissing him on the temple. "Didn't I ask you to join us?"

"The way you said it wasn't exactly inviting."

"Oh, it must have been the phone connection. And what did you do all day?"

"Read ads and wrote letters."

She took the pipe out of his mouth and sucked a puff, letting herself down into his lap and trusting that with just the tiniest bit of luck, they could avoid an argument.

"Wrote letters to whom?" she said.

"Prospective employers … for a part time job, you know. Or don't you remember what we were talking about earlier today?"

"I remember," Kitty said. "Do you feel encouraged about the ads?"

"We'll see."

She snuggled in close and put her arms around his neck. "You write very persuasively," she said. "You'll probably get more offers than you can accept."

"That'll be the day," Fred laughed with a touch of sourness.

"Well, tell me about them." She kissed the side of his neck lightly. "I've got to keep up with things around here."

"Yes, I know," Fred replied. "That's why you run out first thing in the morning."

"Can't we forget it?" Kitty persisted. "Let's just erase today's events and start fresh. I got myself so tangled up today that I can't begin to tell you. And even if I could …"

"Well, you can start by sending that rug back. I know Mark is generous, but this is one thing …."

"I was thinking I'd do exactly that," Kitty said pleasantly. She stuck the pipe stem back between his lips and let her head relax against his chest. "I didn't want that dirty old rug in the first place."

"Well, what did you do with it?"

"Left it in the car. It's too much for me to carry all by myself."

"On the seat?"

"The back seat."

She heard Fred's teeth clamp down on the pipe stem.

"Well, we can't let it sit there all night. I have to go to work in that car." He moved his legs and lifted her gently from his lap. "Come on. I'll carry the damned thing inside for the night anyway."

"That's good. I didn't know what you'd want to do with it."

Kitty went with him to the garage and stood aside while he dragged the rug out of the car and back to the foyer.

He dropped it with a thud just inside the door. "Sounds substantial," he said, "for an old rug."

"Oh, it's that, all right," Kitty said. "You can tell it's a good quality just by the back, the way the knots are done . . . ."

Fred bent over, his eyes focusing with curiosity. "Seems to me the dye came through."

"I think so, but I can't really see it too well in this light."

Fred began pushing it toward the library door.

Kitty switched on the light. "It not only came through on the back," she said, "but it's practically worn out on the front. Just look." She bent over and unrolled it quickly.

The cold wooden floor seemed to come alive with the soft glow of reds and blues, giving the room a point of focus and making of the reading chair an invitation.

Fred stepped back. "Doesn't look so worn to me," he said. "In fact, I kind of like it."

"Do you?"

"Well," he sucked on the pipe thoughtfully and let his eyes roam back to Kitty's face, "for what it cost us, I think it's a damned good buy."

Kitty glanced up and saw on Fred's face a playfulness that she had not seen for a long time.

Fred laughed aloud. "You look like a baby with those round eyes," he said, pulling her to him. "What's with you?"

"Nothing," Kitty said gratefully. "Nothing at all. Just hold me close."

She felt his arms go around her and the steady strength of them. He wasn't angry? Could she dare believe it? She had thought she understood every cog and wheel of Fred's personality, but this quiet acquiescence she had not expected.

"You see," Fred murmured in her ear, "nothing can get me down now. Not rugs. Not Mark's money. Not anything."

He spoke as though he were guarding a special secret and Kitty thrilled at his virile manner.

"Now that I've made up my mind," Fred continued, "I don't feel bogged down by all this foolishness. I can see the light finally. And nothing can stop me now, Kitty."

There was a passion in his voice that sparked Kitty with its electric vitality.

"You really want us to leave this place, don't you?" she murmured.

"We've got to get out. It means our whole lives, Kitty. You see that?"

"I don't know what to believe," Kitty said earnestly. "But if you've made up your mind, I'll go along with it, you know I will."

The sensation of Fred's certainty pumped new life into Kitty's veins and she felt strong and good, sharing his hopes blindly and wanting to believe, as she had once believed in Fred's future and their mutual love.

She lifted her mouth to his and kissed him long and intimately.

"I don't know what to say," Kitty whispered.

"I'll tell you what," Fred smiled. "Make me a sandwich before I starve to death."

Kitty grinned, feeling once more necessary in his life. If it meant a dismal furnished room for Fred to be happy, then she would go there gladly.

Together they went into the kitchen and she fixed him deviled ham with cheese and made a fresh pot of coffee.

"This time next week," he said, "we'll know where we're heading."

She wanted to tell him that next week wasn't important. That it was now that counted. Now. But the idea was merely a vague sensation of yearning that she could not put into words. She knew only that it was late, late in their lives and late in the night. She needed to go to bed and hold him close to her. Feel the breathing and tempo of his spirit next to her own.

While he finished eating, she went into the bedroom and took off her clothing, glad to feel her skin expanding with freedom as she released it from the bondage of underthings. Their brief moment of love making had left memories on her flesh and she wanted him again, longer, more deliberately and with that awareness which makes pleasure so much more poignant.

From the bottom drawer of her dresser she took out a sheer night gown of palest yellow, one that she had not worn for too long, and slipped it over her nakedness. Her breasts tickled beneath the touch of the material and her whole body took up the sensation. She combed out her hair and touched a dab of perfume to her earlobes, smiling all the while with memories.

"What goes here?" Fred said, coming to the doorway.

"Can't you guess?" Kitty said with open pleasure.

"Mmmm."

She turned and held out her arms to him, letting her revealed body invite his gaze.

"Come to me," she said.

She saw him swallow hard and knew that her power to attract him was still as good as new.

"That's my girl," he said and came to take her in his arms.

She felt his tight body going rigid beneath the floppy slacks and heard the gasp of her own voice at the touch of him against her thigh.

She took his hand and led him to the bed, then lay down and closed her eyes.

"Hey, don't fall asleep," Fred bantered.

"Some chance," Kitty laughed, feeling his fingers creeping upward from her knees.

He knew how to touch her.

In the seven years of their marriage, they had learned and perfected delights that had been tossed aside and forgotten for too long.

Kitty craved them now. She wanted everything, the taste, the odor, the touch of him. She wanted to expand and to give, to wring her body dry of its passion and let it flow easily. She wanted to follow again every crevice they had explored in dark and see them lying together in the bright lamplight.

Her hands moved and caught him against the backs of his thighs. Her palms moved along the line of muscle and reached high to the taut curve of his buttocks.

She heard his slacks slip to the floor and then his flesh was against her own, warm and urgent and glad.

"I missed you today," she murmured. "I really did."

"Like hell you did," Fred answered.

She shut the words off with her mouth and found his tongue, taking it in the curling embrace of her own. Her breasts rubbed against the thick hair of his chest, warming as the touch of him ignited twin fires.

His hands cradled her hips and raised them, moving her belly in a circular motion against his. They touched down the full length of each other and she felt him stabbing purposely off base, promising and offering, yet withholding and stimulating thoughts and sensations yet to be tasted.

And again it struck Kitty how incredible it was to be married to this man who could so excite her. Each time it happened like this, it felt to her like riches discovered anew.

She moved her hands to grasp the treasure and know it fully with the blunt focus of recognition.

"Anything you want," she whispered. "I want to be good for you, my darling."

She felt him moving closer, pressing slowly in. She seemed to stretch and envelope him with greedy craving, her hunger yawning and clamping shut like a great mouth.

"Slow," she said, breathing hot vapor against his shoulder. "You know how."

And she felt him moving inside her like no other man could, as though he had mapped the terrain and taken cognizance of all its bypaths.

The speed of him increased and her tempo increased with him, her hips lifting from the mattress to cling even tighter.

"Go ahead," she blurted.

Her direction, releasing him, sent them rapidly uphill, free from the laws of gravitation. Together they floated and Kitty gasped on a dry throat as her craving ballooned, then disappeared behind multicolored clouds.

CHAPTER FIVE

Because Fred wanted it that way, Kitty had an ad put in the local paper.

She had thought that she was ready to go along with Fred's plans. She really wanted to be. Yet, as she peered through the dining room curtains at the first rental prospects, her stomach contracted with cold fury.

They were nice enough looking people. Neatly dressed, obviously established and not too young. Ordinary people ... and she hated them as though they were kidnappers coming to steal her home out from beneath her feet.

She felt her eyelids beginning to tremble and held them tightly shut for an instant, trying to regain control. But the tremor merely turned into a wave of nausea that eddied and swirled.

The doorbell rang.

"Mrs. Miner?"

"Yes. Come in, please. I'm sure you'll like my home. It has ample ..."

She let the speech, prepared in advance, drone on as she took the couple from room to room. Did they have children? Well, that's fine. The school is across and three blocks north ....

They went through the house and left without giving Kitty any commitment.

When she was safely alone, she went into the bathroom and swallowed some aspirin for the headache that had begun to thump beneath the top of her skull.

The afternoon dragged onward as couple after couple looked at the place.

It seemed increasingly incredible to her, as each pair left without making a definite statement, that she was living through the humiliation of it.

A house is not a home, she kept telling herself. But these weren't just any four walls. They had looked hard and long to find this place. And she could not feel convinced that Fred's solution was the only one possible to save them.

The day dragged on, tightening her nerves as it went. She wished that she could talk to Mark or Rose, really open her heart to them. But her problems were nobody's concern. And as she thought of Mark, she felt a flush of embarrassment along her spine. He would have answers, she felt. Too many answers.

She poured a thimbleful of whiskey and drank it down quickly, hoping that it would bolster her morale. She needed strength to face the strangers trespassing through her life. And optimism, too. But optimism was an elusive attribute that seemed to desert her every time she was separated from Fred.

When the doorbell rang again, Kitty was feeling a bit more relaxed.

"I'm Dirk Thornwald," he said, gesturing with an arm that held a folded raincoat. "You have an ad in today's paper?"

"Yes, come in," Kitty said. "Is your wife with you?"

"I'm not married," he smiled. He put the raincoat over the back of a cane chair as though he already lived here.

Kitty realized that she had no real reason to be apprehensive. Yet something about this man made her step back a pace as though she needed distance with which to see him clearly.

"A single man wouldn't want such a large place," she said, feeling helpless, wishing he would leave. "What would you do with eight rooms?"

She tried to laugh politely, but he did not respond. His gray eyes reminded her of Rose's earnest approach to living. They would brook no nonsense, accept nothing phony.

"Well, you see," he said, "I want to open an office in this neighborhood. A medical office."

"Here?"

And now Kitty laughed sincerely. She could hardly visualize her home smelling of alcohol.

"Why not here?" he said seriously. "It's a corner house, the traffic is good. School's close by . . . ."

"Yes, that's true," Kitty admitted. She watched him peripherally while she lit a cigarette to stall for time and self-possession. He had fine, silver blond hair that clung neatly to his well-shaped head. Too tall, too thin, she sensed that he worked hard and that he got poor thanks for his efforts.

"Your first office?" she asked instinctively.

"Yes." He smiled now, shifting his weight and no longer expecting her to invite him to be seated. "At least, on my own."

"Well, I don't know. . . . I hadn't planned, you see." Kitty searched for words. "Doesn't it take a lot of extra plumbing?" she said lamely. "Breaking through walls and floors and all that?"

"Not really," he answered, his eyes taking in the empty whiskey glass and the tilting of Kitty's weight against the door frame. "Dentists need more of that than we do."

"No, I don't think I could allow it."

He studied her for a second. Then he nodded, almost imperceptibly. But the movement of his head told her that he didn't intend to force anything.

"All right," he said and moved to pick up his coat.

"Well, wait a minute," Kitty protested. She hadn't expected him to be willing just to leave it at that. "Besides this matter of plumbing, we didn't intend to give more than a two year lease, you know. I should think that once you got established, you wouldn't want to move from your location."

"Most likely not," he agreed, his eyes leaving her face now and moving around the room. "But I don't try to handle more of my life than I can see in one easy leap."

"That's a good philosophy."

The fear had drained from her and she wondered vaguely what she had expected to happen.

"Come," she offered. "Would you like to look around?"

"Thank you."

She took him, as she had taken the others, on the grand tour. Only this time, she refrained from the rehearsed speech. It could hardly be of interest to him that there was a bar in the basement and a dishwasher and a garbage disposal unit. She really didn't know what to say that could matter and so she said nothing.

"It's a good place," he said behind her. "Lots of windows. I like that."

"And I suppose you would put your office …."

"Downstairs. The steps that lead right down to that separate entrance would make a good place to put up a shingle."

"You seem well organized, Dr. Thornwald."

He grinned with a slightly crooked tilt to his mouth that gave his face an almost rueful expression. "In some respects," he said.

The whiskey had begun to take down Kitty's barriers. "If you want the place, you can have it," she said bluntly. "Frankly, I'm tired of showing it."

"Good. I do like it and I will take it."

Kitty sat down on a chair in the dining room and folded her hands on the lace cloth. Her knuckles seemed red and a bit chapped, she thought. She would have to get a better, more emollient cream.

"I said you were well organized," she smiled.

Thornwald shrugged. His pale face, bony yet soft from the warmth of his expression, bent to Kitty's. "Did your husband leave a lease for us to sign?"

Kitty shook her head.

"Well, I can come back this evening. Or whenever it's most convenient."

He was ready to leave and suddenly she didn't want to part with him. The idea of someone to talk to was far too enticing. Besides, a doctor knew how to be impersonal about things. She could tell him things and he would never repeat them, never condemn her for her weaknesses.

"Would you like a cup of coffee before you go?" she said.

"Yes, I would, thank you."

Kitty nodded and travelled some two inches above the floor on her way to the kitchen.

She wished that she was sober and yet she felt glad that she wasn't quite so. Her tongue felt loose and wiggly. Now that the worst of the business about renting was over, she could take it easier. The demon, stared straight in the face, didn't look so threatening after all.

And a doctor besides.

She felt something of prestige in the lucky stroke that had brought her a doctor. And if he was going to make an office out of the place, he would have to pay more rent than Fred had originally planned to get.

Along with the coffee, she sliced a pecan ring and set it on a good plate.

When she carried it in, Kitty saw that he had made himself comfortable in Fred's reading chair.

"Here's good luck," she said, setting the things down with an exaggerated care.

"And good luck to you, Mrs. Miner," he said, leaning comfortably back and studying her.

For the first time in her life, Kitty felt as though she were being x-rayed right to the heart.

And she hoped fervently that this Dirk Thornwald could discover her trouble and cure it.

CHAPTER SIX

When she told Fred about it, he stared at her with wide, unbelieving eyes.

"Well, for God's sake, what are you looking at me like that for? You'd think I'd rented it out as a brothel or something."

The afternoon's coffee had sobered her, but now she felt that another drink would be good to bolster her against the impending thunder of Fred's objection.

"I don't know what it is about you," he said, pulling off his tie. "But when you come anywhere near the smell of money, you're lost."

"Fred, that's not fair," Kitty said, putting dinner on the table, a meal of sandwiches and soda. "I did very well today and you ought to appreciate it."

"You didn't do much cooking, I can see that," he said with a twist of mock tragedy in his voice.

"I didn't have time," Kitty answered.

Suddenly, she changed her mind about protesting to Fred. A wave of hopelessness drained the energy from her will to fight back at him. She looked around at the star patterned wallpaper and told herself that Fred had no feeling for anything ... not homes or people either. And she felt glad that a person like Dirk Thornwald was coming to live here. He would do right by this place, as Fred never had.

"What are you smiling at?" Fred asked.

His words caught Kitty in the middle of a reverie. She could just see herself married to someone gentle and sensitive ....

Kitty shrugged off the question. "He'll be here in twenty minutes to help draw up the lease."

She felt the headache starting again as she spoke. A small pocket of pain jingled like coins in a purse directly in the center of her skull. She slipped out of the room and poured herself another drink and swallowed it while she gazed out the window and down the street hoping to see a tall, lean figure coming beneath the street lamps.

He would arrive precisely on time, Kitty knew, and she wished Fred would finish eating so she could straighten things up a bit. She heard him coming into the room, munching the last of the sandwich and carrying a glass.

"Say, what are you doing?"

"Nothing," Kitty sighed.

"You know you can't hold that stuff," he said, taking the whiskey glass from her hand.

Kitty turned to him. Her cheeks felt tight and her eyes sharp with anger. "Is there anything you like about me?" she shrilled. "Anything at all?"

It was half a challenge, half a plea for Fred to do something magical.

She dared not tell him, yet she could sense herself drifting away toward someone more congenial.

"Go comb your hair," Fred answered.

Kitty wet her lips. She realized that he hadn't understood her at all.

She carried both their glasses back to the kitchen sink and washed the few things he'd left.

Her heart, a heavy pendulum, swung back and forth with a gloomy rhythmic beat. She could feel the shutters being drawn closed over their married life, the key dropping down a long well never to be regained.

Suddenly, the doorbell rang and she heard the low tone of Dirk's greeting. One hand quickly shot to her blonde hair and she patted it in place, then tested the quality of her lipstick with the point of her tongue before going out to see him.

He looked just as she remembered him ... silvery and calm. Fred, in comparison, seemed like a savage kind of brute.

Kitty introduced them and the three got down to business. Both men, she sensed, wanted to get it over with as soon as possible.

And while they worked on the details, Kitty worked on the liquor bottle. This night, she felt, was a momentous occasion in many ways. For, through the mist of her groggy thoughts, Kitty knew that when they moved out of this house, she would be moving out of Fred's life too. The thought stroked her with sadness and yet she could see that it had been inevitable right from the beginning.

Calmly, she went to sit down and watch them bending over the papers spread out on the dining room table.

And almost before she realized it, Dirk had gone again and she was alone.

He had drifted into her life like a rescue boat coming slowly and carefully through the heavy fog. Yet she knew that she had been waiting for him ... and hoping.

When Fred took her into his arms that night and tried to apologize for his bad temper, Kitty's flesh felt numb to his touch.

"Please," she said, rolling away from him on the bed, "I have a sore throat." She was pushing him out of her life for good, but trying to do it gently, so that he would not question.

"You know, Kitty, I have to admit that you were right. I've been thinking about it and it won't be so bad, letting a doctor have this place."

"Kind of late to think about it now," she said dully, "after it's all been done."

She had not meant to hurt him, yet the sharpness in her tone could have cut through the hide of an elephant.

"Say, what's the matter with you, anyway," he said, reaching out a hand to stroke her shoulder.

"I told you. I don't feel too well."

She spoke the truth, yet at the same time, it was not really the truth. Her ability to manufacture things had created the sore throat and aching head.

Fred kissed her gently on the cheek.

"Let's not fight," he said.

"I'm not fighting, dear. I just don't feel well."

His arms reached across the pillow and tried to draw her close. "Can I help?" he said.

Kitty heard the slight hoarseness in his voice that told her of things subtly on his mind. She remembered how good their love making had been and she let his hands find and hold one breast beneath the loose fitting nightgown.

But tonight, his touch did not soothe her. The love she had felt for Fred seemed lost in the jungle of other emotions. Resentment began to stir in her as his hands searched over her body. If he loved her, why was he always criticizing her efforts?

Kitty tried to pull away, but only with half a heart. Her body seemed not to care about the muddled thoughts in her brain; her flesh responded with a mind of its own. She lay still, breathing quietly and trying to surpress the insistent desire.

"Please, dear," she murmured. "Not now." Her voice, lacking conviction, trembled along the pillow case and faded.

The shadowed outline of her husband's head rose above her own. She saw the profile of his mouth and the slight flaring of his nostrils and knew that he did not believe her any more than she believed herself.

His lips plunged and found the hollow of her throat.

Unwillingly, her arms moved to caress the hard curve of his shoulders and the strength of his narrowing back. She felt the animal desires in him vibrating, calling to her.

"I need you," he muttered and the warm vapor of his breath slid across her bosom.

The anger and the hurt that she had nurtured began to dissolve. She gazed beyond the windows at the silhouettes of other houses down the street and wondered if people behind those darkened curtains were as restless and confused as she.

"Darling, be good to me," she said with an anguished cry, praying that Fred would understand her needs and make life simple.

His lips roamed over her body, grazing along the curves of her flat stomach and over her hips. She could feel that he was searching for her, for her response and for her loving. His chin, roughened since the morning's shave, bruised and the burning sensation felt oddly pleasant. There was no such thing as pure pleasure for her, only pleasure mingled with pain, as though to balance her seesaw of craving.

The struggle to remain aloof from Fred subsided like a tired enemy. She could not avoid him, could not fight him off. Not now, anyway, while their bodies touched, almost shyly at first.

Fred cradled her in his arms and she knew that he would not try to force her. His barrel chest and tight hips could overwhelm her and take what he wanted. But he was holding off, keeping himself away as though waiting for her consent. And Kitty felt grateful.

"Play with me," she whispered, needing and wanting attention as much as his love.

His willing hands stroked and fondled. He seemed like a great bear trying to be gentle.

Impulsively, Kitty kissed his arm. She felt warm and secure like this. If only the feeling could last forever.

"Are you okay?" Fred asked as though he intuited her feelings.

"Yes." There seemed nothing else to say that hadn't already been gone over a thousand times. It was useless to make Fred see that they could never be of one mind.

Useless … and unnecessary, too, at this moment while their craving for fulfillment bubbled up.

Kitty opened herself to him and invited the thrilling oblivion that would deny all trouble.

She felt him settle and glide easily to possess her. The sweet poignancy drove off all sense. She knew only of the maleness taking her and of her own abandon. A delicious yielding swam through her veins, making her body soft and tractable. She felt that every bone had melted and that she could twist and bend herself into any position that pleased.

The tempo of him increased. Their mingling became a melody surging into the crashing chords that blended and spread across the whole orchestra of her nerves.

"Oh, darling," she muttered and closed her eyes to the light of consummation.

Then silently, like the rolling of mist over hills, Kitty fell asleep, to dream again of her pleasure and the secret thrills of loving.

CHAPTER SEVEN

Kitty awoke after Fred had already left for the office.

She reached across the mattress, groping for him, needing his nearness and finding only the empty expanse of bed.

Slowly, she opened her eyes. The room was a rumple of clothing that he had left behind. Brush and comb lay scattered on the bureau, his pajama bottoms hung halfway off the bed.

Kitty sighed. She could sense Fred's vitality, but she could not help feeling that somehow he had deserted her.

Tiredly, she climbed out of bed. Her nightgown lay draped on one bedpost and she stood for a while, studying her nakedness that had been so satisfying during the night.

Now she was merely a bundle of oppressions. Restless and without a steadying arm to guide her, she fell prey to random thoughts moving toward hate.

She brushed her teeth briskly and tried to pick up her spirits by eating a solid breakfast. Still, loneliness ebbed and flowed around her, calm as a lagoon and deep.

On the dining room table, she found the duplicate copy of the lease and began to read it just for something to do. The day around her, empty of meaning and purpose, swelled like an infected wound.

As she set down the lease, she noticed a scrap of paper with Fred's handwriting on it.

PHONE THORNWALD AND MAKE ARRANGE-
MENTS ABOUT PAINTING.

Fred had not even bothered to sign his name, taking her for granted, making her feel invisible again or like some lackey in his employ.

But anger did not rush to consume her this time. Instead, she felt a strange thrill creeping up to tickle her lips and soon she realized that she was smiling.

Dirk Thornwald's phone number was scribbled in pencil on the lease. It was a city number and it seemed to her that it might be nice to live in the city again, where the people were, if one had someone like Dirk....

She dialled and waited and when he answered made an appointment for him to come out early that afternoon.

After she had hung up, Kitty pranced to the closet and busied herself with making a selection. She took out a green dress, one that clung to her and that Fred hated. It was practically new. Neglected. She slipped it on and considered the reflection of herself in the dresser mirror.

It seemed to her that Fred's taste was all in his mouth. He just didn't appreciate the finer things in life, like the way this dress showed off her figure. He liked her well enough naked beside him in bed. But during the daytime? Go through the streets like a nun. Cover those curves. Hide your light under a tent....

Well, she didn't intend to hide her light today. Or any other day, ever again, for that matter.

Angrily, she went to the closet once more and chose the highest heels she could find. She had good legs and the curve of her instep belonged in high heels.

The idea is for a woman to be feminine. It's a compliment to men. Why doesn't Fred see it that way, too?

The exasperation of her troubles hit Kitty hard. Every other man in the world liked the way she looked, but not her own husband.

She rubbed pomade onto the ends of her hair and brushed the deep blonde waves sleekly upward, pinning them with a silver bar at the very crown of her head. Then, needing the color of a tea rose to give her appearance that final lift, she called the florist and ordered a dozen.

By the time Dirk Thornwald arrived, Kitty's home smelled of roses and glowed with her own satisfaction.

"I'm sorry I had to drag you all the way out here," she said, not feeling sorry in the least.

Dirk set his fedora into her waiting hands and smiled with the silvery, elusive smile she remembered so clearly.

"I'm not sorry at all," he said.

Kitty felt herself blush warmly in tiny spots of color high on her cheeks.

"I see you've been living on Madison Avenue," she said, noting how the blue of his tie gave a certain depth and definition to his eyes. "Somehow, I'd gotten the impression you were a country boy."

"Not at all, Kitty," he said easily.

She felt herself jolted at his use of her first name and decided right then that she would ask him to stay to lunch after such a long ride.

"In fact," he went on, "this will be my first time really out of New York."

She led him to the living room and fixed highballs. She kept a casual manner, as though they had known each other for years. "What made you decide on the suburbs?" she asked conversationally.

Dirk took the glass and settled down, balancing it above his crossed legs and watching her calmly. His eyes seemed to be probing her today ... and not professionally. She could feel that he was judging the cut and cling of her dress, the way she swayed when she crossed the thick pile carpet. He seemed to be looking with a steady glance right down to the bottom of her deepest secrets ... and finding them not so terrible at all.

"It was an easy decision, really," Dirk said, "when you consider the competition in Manhattan."

Kitty laughed between sips of her own drink. She was not accustomed to taking liquor so early in the day. But then again, she wasn't accustomed to many things that had begun to happen to her lately.

"The competition is pretty stiff out here, too, you know," she said casually.

Her words took on a queer double meaning and she glanced quickly away from him to the dark blue knit of his socks.

"But I'm bothering you with too many questions," she said quickly, to hide her embarrassment. "I don't know what you had in mind about the decorating. Would you like to tell me?"

"Frankly," Dirk said, shrugging his shoulders, "that kind of thing leaves me at a loss. I was sort of hoping that you might give me some suggestions. If you have the time, that is."

"Oh, I have time," Kitty said with a bitter twist to her lips.

She saw one blond eyebrow go up in sudden alertness, as though like a lion he had caught a whiff of tender meat on the air.

"Frankly, though," she hurried on, "I would suggest a plain bone white throughout. It has a dignity colors don't give."

"Dignity," he echoed. "Is that what you think the place needs?"

"Well, a professional man," Kitty waved her glass helplessly. "Yes, I think dignity is very important, don't you?"

Dirk shook his head. "Nope. I think it's overestimated," he said. "Dignity. Prestige. Gobbledegook."

"Oh. Then I suppose you do have some strong ideas, after all, don't you, Dr. Thornwald?"

"My name is Dirk."

She had wanted to keep the safety of distance between them by using his last name. But she realized now that it was foolish.

He wouldn't permit it and besides, the result of her effort had been stupid and artificial.

"Dirk," she repeated, liking the way her lips had to pucker to say it. Yes, saying his name was like getting ready to be kissed.

Still, she couldn't just sit here, gazing at him like a child. Embarrassment moved her to action. "We ought to go to a paint store and look at some samples," she said lamely, not knowing what to say that would cover her awkwardness.

"I didn't intend to put you to all that trouble," Dirk said.

"You aren't," she answered softly, forgetting about luncheon. "I enjoy any excuse to get out and be in the world."

She spoke frankly because Dirk wouldn't swallow her phoniness. And as she talked, she went to get a short jacket, then turned to follow him outside.

"We can use my car," Kitty said.

"We'll have to," Dirk smiled. "I didn't bring one."

He was sensible and direct and Kitty began to sense that she would always know exactly where she stood with Dirk Thornwald. Unlike Fred, there was no blowing hot or cold according to temper.

"You know what I'd like," Kitty said impulsively when they had pulled out onto the street.

"What?" Dirk said, making his voice a subtle goad of encouragement.

"To go in to one of the larger stores in New York. Where we'll have a better selection ...."

"Fine with me."

Swiftly, Kitty got the car onto the highway before her dream could burst and remind her that this was just a tenant and she just a landlady. It was pleasanter to feel that they were headed, not for business, but for a sociable afternoon.

Dirk's presence beside her felt reassuring. Kitty kept reminding herself that this man was a different species from Fred. As a doctor, he would be objective, understanding, able to appreciate the delicacy of life's demands.

"What colors do you have in your office now?" Kitty said into the friendly silence.

"Pale blues," Dirk answered.

"Would you like something like that again?"

Dirk rolled down the window and leaned against it, folding his arms across his jacket. "No, I've had enough of it. I'm looking for a complete change, you see."

"Aren't we all?" Kitty said philosophically.

"Yes. At first I thought you weren't so anxious to rent your place out," he said. "I had the feeling of being an intruder."

"Well, in a sense you are," Kitty said, keeping her eyes on the road. "But a nice one."

She heard Dirk grunt as though he had diagnosed her meaning and expected it to be curable.

"But I'm beginning to look forward," Kitty continued. "We're moving into the city. My husband and I."

"I see."

"Yes. The other day I thought I'd never be able to get used to the idea again and now I'm really anxious. There are so many things to do that I've been missing. And I've only just begun to realize it."

"Like what, for example?"

"Oh, the theater, the latest art shows."

"Is that really what you've been missing?"

His question hit home like a surgeon's scalpel.

"Well, you don't expect a person to come right out and say things," Kitty blurted. She felt safe, clinging to the wheel and feeling the stable weight of the car beneath her. No matter what she said, she felt confident that she would not cause trouble. Even if she were awkward or too frank, Dirk would interpret her meaning precisely as she intended.

"May I offer a suggestion?" Dirk said after a long pause.

"Anything."

"It's simply this," Dirk said. "Do whatever you feel you must, Kitty. But remember that each of us has to pay a price for whatever it is we want in life."

His advice seemed to Kitty more like a riddle. "I don't really want anything at all, Dirk."

"That couldn't be true," he answered immediately. "Each of us wants some one thing deeply. Only, some of us haven't quite uncovered what that one thing is."

"And you?" Kitty said, needing to evade the spotlight for a moment. "Are you paying the price for some certain something?"

Dirk stretched his legs. "Indeed I am, Kitty," he said quietly.

"And what is it, pray tell?"

"Not now," Dirk smiled. "On such a beautiful day, you don't want to hear about my trouble."

Kitty felt a strong desire to protest and an even stronger curiosity. Yet it would not be good manners to try to force him to speak. He seemed now not only a doctor, but a man of mystery who piques the attention with the kind of harmless yet intense interest that Kitty had experienced before only in the movies.

Fred was as bright and as obvious as the scenery whizzing by. And she had not known many others before their marriage.

By contrast, Dirk seemed like a bag of treasures with the string pulled tight. She wanted to loosen that string and peek in. Just once.

"Let's go to your office," Kitty said when they arrived in Manhattan. "I'd like to get an idea of your taste in decor."

CHAPTER EIGHT

She caught sight of his shingle from across Park Avenue and it struck Kitty that just yesterday he had told her the new office would be the first on his own. Yet his name was the only one listed beside the building door.

It was a big old building, quite substantial, obviously expensive to live in and in one of the best neighborhoods for medical practice.

Dirk's fingers touched her elbow and led her across through traffic. They climbed the three steps to his office door and went inside to an empty waiting room with worn leather seats and beyond that, a consultation room, very large and filled with leather bound books. On the walls, old letters with famous signatures hung in narrow black frames. A hand carved globe stood on a mahogany table and beside it, an ancient microscope, its gold tarnished, tilted on display.

"This is a very lovely office," Kitty breathed.

The place felt mellow and solid, its dark rust rug and rust colored curtains giving her the sensation of being inside a huge polished barrel.

"Yes, I like it," Dirk said, taking her jacket and folding it carefully before he draped it over the wide wing chair opposite an expanse of desk that commanded the room.

"And you want to move?" Kitty asked innocently and painfully curious.

"I want to move," Dirk repeated.

He said nothing to amplify it and Kitty waited as long as she could before the demands of courtesy made her change the subject.

"I don't see those pale blues you were talking about," she offered with a businesslike manner to cool off her heated interest in his private affairs.

"That's in the operating room," he said, turning over a blank page in an appointment book to one with the day's date on it. "Would you like to see?"

"Of course," Kitty smiled. "Isn't that what I came for?"

She saw his mouth crinkle slightly in one corner as thought he were about to question this statement. But he held back.

He took her into an adjoining room where the walls were done in blue and the moldings in a deep ivory. The familiar antiseptic odor and the gleam of instruments laid out on towels in a cabinet made Kitty remember suddenly that she hadn't been feeling too well.

"I wonder," she said on a whim. "As long as we're here ... if you wouldn't look at me ... at my throat. I've been fighting a cold this past week, but it seems to be hanging on and on."

"Why, of course," Dirk said.

For an instant she thought that his voice was mocking her, yet it couldn't be, for her request was sincere.

"Won't you sit up there on the table?"

With a sprightly movement, Kitty hopped up to comply. She sat there watching him take a wooden tongue depressor from a container of them and enjoying the promise of attention.

Then he came in very close and she could smell the faint odor of his shaving lotion that seemed to be emanting from his clothes.

"Open your mouth."

Obediently, Kitty opened and said *ahhh* as she had learned to do in her childhood. And she felt very young as Dirk peered down her throat, his forehead wrinkling and serious, his eyes focused on something way back in her throat.

Without comment, he proceeded through the ritual of examination. The cold touch of metal to her heart and the bright pin point of light in one eye, then the other seemed like a little game of hide and seek with Dirk the seeker and her body the hidden one.

He put the instruments into the sterilizer and set a stethoscope around his neck.

"Open your blouse, please."

With a thrill of horror, Kitty remembered that there was more to an examination than she had intended. But she dared not stop now, dared not let him realize that she was not as serious about her health as he.

"Well, couldn't you see anything so far?" Kitty said, stalling for time.

"Open your blouse, please."

There was nothing to do but obey.

With trembling fingers, Kitty opened the first two buttons. He went around behind her and helped lift the material free from her skirt. She felt the touch of his fingers below her shoulder blades. A steady coolness seemed to be coming from him as though he were all brains and no feeling. Yet his hand seemed to experience her with a knowledge so personal, so profoundly intimate that Kitty wanted to cry.

"Open your mouth and breathe deeply ... breathe ... breathe."

Kitty tried to breathe in rhythm to his command, but the wild pounding where her heart should have been made a normal response impossible.

The mouth of the stethoscope moved along her just as Fred's lips had touched her, in private places. Time seemed to stand solidly still, refusing to move onward, as Dirk listened to her heart and to her lungs.

When he had finished, he folded the stethoscope and put it back into the small black bag.

"You know what's the matter with you, young lady?" Dirk said.

Kitty shook her head. He seemed suddenly too serious, too intent. She wished she had not started all of this in the first place and her hands leaped to cover her body that he had touched and seen.

"Boredom," he said flatly. "An acute case of boredom brought on by nothing to do."

Kitty flew from the examining table.

"That's rude of you," she said, not knowing where to hide.

"Rude, perhaps. But clinically true and truth is all I can offer you, Kitty. Will you listen?"

"There's nothing for me to hear, if that's all the sense you can make, Dr. Thornwald. I hope you don't treat all your patients with the same nonchalance."

"I treat each as best I can," Dirk said with a steadiness that told Kitty her words had left him unimpressed. "But getting back to you. If I were really your doctor and if I could get you to listen to me, I'd prescribe a good dose of steady work at something that interests you ... all of you, for a change, instead of just the skim top of your mind."

"Thank you for nothing," Kitty said.

Dirk shrugged. "You're very welcome."

She had her clothes straightened, but she didn't feel any better for it. If she could leap from the window and run far away. Forget that there had ever been such a horrible man as this one who still stared at her with no-nonsense eyes, as though he enjoyed not giving her a single moment's mercy.

"We'd better attend to the paint," Kitty said, finding a last thread to cling to. "Shall we be dressed and going?"

"I'm quite ready," Dirk said. "It was your idea to come here in the first place, remember?"

"Well, I've seen enough. I've certainly seen enough," Kitty said breathlessly, talking half to him, but mostly to her own conscience that seemed to be hovering in a state of commotion right over her forehead like an old maid aunt.

Dirk went to a basin, washed his hands and dried them slowly on a white folded towel.

"We'll have some lunch first," he said, "before we make the rounds."

It wasn't an invitation ... or a question, either. Kitty heard in his voice a command that told her what she was going to do next. It burned her with a fury, as though this man could sit down with the greatest of ease and plan out the rest of her life for her in complete detail.

"All right," Kitty said, needing to fling some of the mud back. "We'll have some lunch."

But she couldn't quite get the degree of control over her tone to do him any damage. And all of her wanted to reach out and claw the skin off his face.

"You're rather flushed," Dirk said calmly as they proceeded back to the consultation room and he handed her her jacket. "Have I offended you?"

"Of course not," Kitty replied, making of her voice a whip. "How could I be offended by a ...."

She could not find the word.

And as though Dirk himself could reach up to a top shelf and take it down for her, she gazed up the many inches to his face.

As she gazed at him, she saw in his tired face only kindness. She had wanted to dislike him, to be aloof and therefore protected from his opinion. But none of these things could she accomplish. Instead, she felt like the world was made of glass and threatening to topple at her feet any instant.

"Dirk," she said, "Dirk ... please help me."

He sat her down in the chair and pulled another one up close. "What can I do?" he said gently. "People who are spoiled have the worst time of it in this world. I know. One becomes accustomed to all the best cuts of cake and when they stop coming our way ...."

"Am I spoiled?" Kitty said. "You know, I don't feel spoiled."

"I don't really know, do I? What do I know about you at all, Kitty Miner, except that you are unhappy with no obvious reason to be. Is there a reason?"

"Isn't there always?"

"Well, there are reasons and reasons. Some are quite incurable. I hope yours isn't." He reached to a humidor and lifted a pipe from the rack beside it.

"Well, as soon as I leave Fred, I'll be cured, that's for sure."

"I see."

"No, you don't, Dirk. You probably think I'm crazy."

"Why should I think such a thing?"

She watched a match flame suck down into the pipe bowl and rise again. "Why shouldn't you?"

"Well, for one thing, we hardly know each other."

The words surprised Kitty. She felt as though they had known each other all their lives. But it was true. He knew nothing of her at all. Not her past, only one small fragment of her present ... and certainly nothing of her hopes for the future.

But did she want him to know these things? He was like soft, white wool that she wanted to tangle around her and play with as a kitten in front of a hearth. She wanted her life to be a fairy tale that he would help to create.

And if she told him all the ugly truths, how could he possibly make her life like any of the happier stories she would have preferred?

"You don't want to know about me, Dirk. And I don't want to tell you," she said earnestly.

"Then there's no use, is there?"

He spoke matter of factly, no urgency asking her to reveal herself, no curiosity tempting her.

"Maybe we'd better get that lunch," Kitty said, slipping into her jacket and swallowing hard to steady herself for facing the crowds outside and her responsibility to them to put on her best face.

CHAPTER NINE

"I'll tell you about myself then," Dirk said as they sat facing each other in a restaurant crowded with lunch hour traffic.

Kitty listened to his history, how he had been in service and started his education there, stories about his family in the Midwest, the sheep farm they now lived on.

She listened attentively to it all, expecting at any moment for the heroine to enter. But Dirk made no mention of girls. She wondered, as she ate her soup, whether he had left out the romance part purposely as a courtesy to her or if there simply hadn't been any important women in his life.

Studying his blond good looks, she found this thought hard to believe. And yet, medical men worked hard. They had little time for such things as love, she had heard. And enjoying good times on the run, well … that was part of the profession.

"Whenever you're thinking hard," Dirk interrupted her, "you look like a little monkey I used to know who sat behind the bars of his cage waiting for a piece of ham sandwich. Little Joe absolutely loved ham sandwiches."

"You are all full of compliments, aren't you, Dirk," Kitty said wryly.

Her swift anger with him had subsided, leaving a residue of pleasure that felt like a rainbow after a summer shower.

"I guess I never learned the finer graces," he said.

The waiters and people dashing around them seemed to create a private island of their table. Kitty felt that they were sitting in the center of a stormy sea, encased in a glass dome permitting entry only of food and drink.

Nothing could hurt her now.

She had not told Dirk the details of her life, but she felt confident that he understood, that he had drained the meaning from her implications. In time, he would stop chiding her and lend a sympathetic ear. Doctors were like that sometimes .. they liked to minimize the trouble in the hope that it would die simply of inanition.

Boredom, indeed.

She dared not reveal exactly how bored she really was.

How Fred bored her with continuous plans that always exploded into a deeper tangle than the one before.

How saving money bored her because one could never save enough to make it feel worthwhile.

How the sight of her own image bored her because deep down inside, she could never quite feel worthwhile.

"Shall we go?" Dirk said just as she finished her second cup of coffee.

He wasn't one to waste words or time and Kitty felt that she would have to learn to get used to this about him.

The afternoon sped pleasantly; they went from one store to the next, collecting folders of sample colors and studying them as they strolled the streets.

It felt as though they were planning to do an apartment together and Kitty felt a creeping up of intimacy between them that she dared not put into words.

At the end of the day, she drove Dirk back to his office and took herself home alone, her mind pleasantly aired with fresh experiences, things to think about and try to understand as she went about the routine business of preparing for her evening with Fred.

Fred ....

His name and the expectation of him hit Kitty in the face like a slap of cold water. Somehow, she had managed to put him off, as though he were an old dress that she didn't want to be seen wearing.

When she heard his key in the lock, her back tightened with apprehension. She felt afraid of what her face would show to him, what her eyes would reveal of the distances away from him and their marriage she had travelled this afternoon.

"So there," Fred announced, bursting into the kitchen and kissing her on the nape of the neck. "Congratulate me."

"For what?" Kitty said flatly.

"My last day on the job."

"Congratulations."

Fred opened the refrigerator door and peered in. "You don't exactly sound like a cheering squad."

"Should I?"

"Of course," Fred said, his chest expanding as he lifted a bottle of milk to his lips. "It isn't every day that a man climbs out from a rut that's deeper than his own head."

"Well, you dug it yourself," Kitty replied, slicing carrots with venomous energy.

"Maybe. But I got out of it myself, too. So sound a little pleased, anyway."

"I'm pleased. Will you put the butter on the table?"

Kitty felt rather than heard Fred's pause. It was as though he had squatted down to peer at the little insects crawling out from the underside of a stone.

"Are you all right, Kitty?" he said after a while.

"Yes. Quite fine."

Another silence.

Fred brought silver and napkins to the table and then came to stand beside her at the sink.

"And how did you spend your day?" he asked.

She knew that he just wanted to make pleasant conversation. That she should have given him at least a few words of praise. That his disappointment in her response hung just behind the eagerness in his eyes.

"Just as you told me to," Kitty said coolly.

She glanced at him and saw the puzzlement wrinkling across the bridge of his nose. "What did I tell you to?" he said.

"To see about the painting for our new tenant."

"Oh, that."

She realized that he had forgotten the whole business. Kitty turned on hot water and washed grease from her fingers. Wouldn't he be surprised to find out that there were things he'd better not forget if he knew what was good for him?

Still, she decided not to tell him about her day. Why make an important thing of it?"

It wasn't important.... Fred had been right.... Just a business engagement ... a petty detail....

Her heart fluttered at the thought of Dirk, his steady fingers moving the stethoscope over the flesh of her left breast. She recalled how he had slipped it beneath the swell of her flesh and listened and how the metal had grown warmer from her own body heat.

Important?

Kitty smiled to herself. It felt good, suddenly, to have secrets from Fred. And it served him right.

"Know what we're going to do tomorrow?" he said.

His voice filtered through the maze of her thoughts. She seemed to be floating a great distance above his head and the sight of him was like a tiny speck of earth that was wind blown, that could be ground under foot without a moment's consideration.

"What are we going to do?" Kitty said, trying to sound interested.

"Well," he leaned against the sink, "since it's my first free day, I thought we'd go to the city and have ourselves a good time. Sort of a celebration, you know. The movies. Dinner. Dancing in the evening. Would you like that?"

Kitty dried her hands and carried the freshly made salad to the table. She began sprinkling vinegar and oil over the crisp leaves and watched the liquid slide down the crinkly sides.

"I don't know," she sighed. "I feel so tired these days. Couldn't we make it another time?"

As Kitty pulled in her chair, she dared not face Fred, directly across from her. If she looked into his eyes, she knew her soul would well right up into them and he would see that she had no interest whatsoever in going anyplace with him ... ever again.

The quality in Fred that had once thrilled her and made life sparkle had somehow gotten lost. And as she cut into her steak, Kitty realized that she wouldn't know where to look to find it and what was more, that she didn't care.

CHAPTER TEN

"But we have to find a place to live." *Whose side are you on,* his voice seemed to say. *What are you trying to do to us?*

"I don't see why we have to go apartment hunting this very minute," Kitty answered irritably.

He was beginning to get on her nerves. One day home and he hung around her, sticking like fly paper.

"The longer we wait, the less choice we'll have that's all," Fred said. He had rolled up the stretched sleeves of a sweatshirt and his bare arms hanging out reminded Kitty of a gesticulating ape.

"I don't feel quite right," she said. "If you had any consideration at all, you'd wait until my throat felt better or go look by yourself."

She had been unable to look him square in the eyes ever since last night and she knew that soon he would realize that all wasn't going quite as he had planned.

"If you're ill," Fred said with a suddenly subdued tone, "we ought to take you to a doctor."

"I don't need one, thank you," Kitty snapped, closing the book she had been vainly trying to read. "A little rest and quiet will do just fine."

"Seems to me," Fred bent to the television set and began flipping over channels, "all you ever do is rest and have quiet."

His voice accused her and Kitty jumped as though a hot metal rod had been stuck through her chest.

"I don't know why you men think a woman is supposed to do a thousand jobs all at the same time. How would you feel if you had to work and take care of a house, too?"

"Doesn't seem to me that I see much house cleaning done around here."

Fred's voice unerringly picked out all the little housekeeping details that Kitty had been neglecting.

"Is that what you think?"

"And if you want me to add more," Fred's voice rose in parallel with Kitty's, "I don't mind telling you that I'm sick of sandwiches and soup for supper."

He struck his knee a blow that Kitty recognized as finality.

It was the signal for a door to open. For his temper to break loose. But this time, Kitty knew that she wasn't going to cajole him. She had had enough of taking his meanness and trying to twist it with a sweet tact into something bearable to live with.

She stood up abruptly and let the book fall to the floor.

"If that's how you feel, you should have told me sooner," she replied without raising her voice. "But even now, it's not too late."

Marching into the bedroom, she got her raincoat and buttoned it on.

"And just where are you going?" Fred demanded as she passed him on the way to the door.

Kitty had never felt calmer in her life. A decision had been made deep within her, one that had not asked either her opinion or her consent.

"Away from you," she said. "And away from all this bickering that's been ruining us both."

She did not wait for him to reply, but sailed out the door and into her car, not quite certain where she would go, but certain with a rocklike strength that she would never come back again.

She did not even turn around to see if he were standing, puzzled, at the doorway.

The key turned in the ignition and Kitty drove off smoothly, heading into the night and into the new story that she would write for herself. Only this one, she determined, would have a happier ending.

For a while she drove aimlessly, letting the wind take her blonde hair and blow it like a proud flag. She seemed to be moving in a dream, hardly aware of what she had done. Only one thing did she care about and that was to show Fred how much she disapproved of his methods. He had treated her all these years as though she had no mind of her own. Whatever he believed, she had to believe. Whatever he wanted, she had to want.

Well, those days were over.

She would live for herself alone now. Perhaps find the purpose in life that Dirk had told her each person must have.

With no one next to her to argue away her convictions, Kitty felt stronger than she had ever felt before. The more she considered this, the more directly her car headed toward Long Island and the comforting companionship of her sister. Kitty felt certain that Rose would give her encouragement. Not that she needed it just yet. She felt too new, too full of steam and energy.

Start something with force and it practically finishes itself, carried along on the stream and current of its own energy. Kitty felt like a light canoe bobbing down a boiling river. She could see the dangers ahead, but she also felt that she could maneuver through them.

By the time she drove into Rose's three car garage, Kitty felt that she already had all the answers.

Rose answered the bell and greeted Kitty with happy surprise.

Kitty waited till she had come inside and Rose had settled her with a cup of tea. Then she said, "I want you to know something. I've left Fred."

She watched Rose's interest flicker, then the eyes revealed a disappointment, a sadness that unnerved Kitty.

"What's the matter with you?" Kitty asked, nibbling one of Rose's homemade cookies. "You look as though it were the end of the world."

Rose took a tangerine from a crystal bowl and began to peel it slowly. "What's the matter with you that you sound so pleased with yourself?"

"Well, nobody likes to see a marriage go on the rocks," Kitty admitted. "But you're supposed to be glad for me, Rose, that I had the strength to do it, to pick myself up and call it quits."

"I don't see why that takes strength," Rose answered blandly. "Any little child can run away from home. And so many do."

"Is that what you think?"

Kitty's own disappointment overwhelmed her now. She felt sure that Rose must be prejudiced, perhaps old fashioned about such things as the sacredness of the home.

"I've always known you to be self centered and impulsive, Kitty. But I've always had the faith that you would never do anything drastic."

"Fred believes in drastic action. You heard him that night. Why shouldn't I?"

"Well, never mind," Rose sighed. "You can stay with us. We have plenty of room until the boys come home. And then we'll manage other arrangements. Let's bring in your valises."

"I don't have any," Kitty said.

Rose's smooth face tightened with curiosity. "You mean, you simply walked out," she said, "without so much as a toothbrush."

"No. The toothbrush I have," Kitty laughed. "But that's about all."

Rose pushed up one sleeve of her cashmere sweater and nodded. "For a moment there, I was taking you seriously, Kitty." Her voice, obviously relieved, lilted now.

"But I am serious," Kitty scowled with annoyance. "I don't have to cart out sofas to convince you, do I? Besides, we've already rented the place. There isn't much to take."

"And your clothing?"

"Most of it is dowdy old stuff that nobody but Fred likes anyhow."

In Rose's vast living room, Kitty's voice sounded lost. It seemed to creep around the piano and melt silently into the heavy drapes and the wall to wall carpeting. Nothing could be too problematical in a room like this. It seemed to reach around and protect one like a mother hen.

Kitty snuggled down into the over-stuffed chair and closed her eyes, recalling Dirk and feeling his reaction to her move. Would he still be so professional, she wondered? Would he have to remain aloof from her, now that she had separated from Fred?

It posed an interesting question in Kitty's mind. One that she intended to experiment with and answer.

"For the time being," Rose said, "I'll go along with you, Kitty. But I don't want any trouble from you, please."

"What kind of trouble?" Kitty laughed, feeling divested of all her burdens and twenty pounds lighter.

"I want you to make yourself useful and try to keep happy."

Kitty pursed her lips with impatience. "Everyone seems to be saying that to me these days."

"Who's everybody?"

Kitty hesitated. She wanted to tell Rose about Dirk, yet she felt afraid that Rose's reaction might not please her.

"Just everybody," she said.

"Well, come, let me show you your room so you can get comfortable."

"Room?" Kitty looked at her questioningly.

"Yes. Where you'll sleep."

Kitty took a cigarette and lit it with a heavy silver lighter from the table. It was carved in the shape of a wild duck and she knew that this would be Mark's masculine taste. It felt nice to remember Mark and to know that Dirk was like him in some ways. In his steadiness, for example.

"I'm not sleeping here, Rose," Kitty smiled. "But thank you, anyhow."

"Of course you are," Rose said abruptly. "I won't have it any other way."

"You know, you look just like Momma when you try to be imperious," Kitty said, observing the light on Rose's silver hair and the angle at which her head balanced on the slender throat.

"Don't get off the subject," Rose persisted. "Where will you go if you don't stay here with us?"

"To a hotel," Kitty answered easily. "The city is full of them."

"A hotel? But why, for heaven's sake?"

Rose's question hit Kitty in a delicate area. She wasn't sure herself quite why. After all, if she intended to see Dirk, she could do so from Rose's home. There was nothing dishonorable about it, after all. As his landlady, she might have to see him from time to time anyhow. But still, there was something in her that needed privacy, that wanted to be completely independent and alone with itself. She could almost feel that there were corners in her soul that she had never explored and that she must discover now, before it was too late. And this kind of searching was something she needed to do by herself, without anyone's help or advice or experience.

"Sometimes a person just has to be by himself," Kitty said simply. "Please don't argue with me, Rose. I'm in no mood for it."

"Perhaps Mark can convince you," Rose said quietly.

There was something peculiar in the way she said it that made Kitty stare at her with a new curiosity. Was it a bitter twinge? Kitty could not be sure.

"What has Mark got to do with this?" Kitty asked bluntly.

"Mark understands women, you know," Rose answered. "He'll probably understand you and dissuade you from your plans."

"But why should he?"

"Why, indeed?" Rose echoed.

Kitty leaned forward in her chair and her fingers tightened on the handle of the delicate porcelain cup. "Rose, what are you trying to tell me? Now, speak out."

"Well, you spent a day alone with Mark. You should be able to tell me."

"Tell you …."

The two women stared at each other for a while in silence. The family resemblance between them seemed to strengthen as each sat quietly looking at the other.

Then Kitty broke the silence by getting up from her chair and going to Rose. She sat down on the wide arm of the sofa and leaned to put her arm around Rose's narrow and graceful shoulder.

"Now, come along," Kitty urged gently. "And tell me everything. I haven't the faintest idea of what you're trying to say, but I want to understand."

She heard her sister let out a breath of resignation and felt her stalwart, proud posture slump ever so slightly.

"You really don't know, then?" Rose said dully.

"Of course not. How could I?"

But Kitty was beginning to suspect and the cold fingers of dread started to grip her across the belly. She managed, however, to keep the nonchalant innocence of a smile on her face. A camouflage that was to fool the world that everything terrible in life could be met and overcome. It was something she fervently wished were true, and something she often felt was further from truth than anything else.

"Mark isn't exactly what one would call a homebody," Rose began. "If you know what I mean. And when he stepped out this past Sunday, I simply took it for granted that he wasn't … well, on a business trip. Then it turned out to be you he had spent the day with and, Kitty, you can't imagine how frightened I was that Mark had tried to make a fool of himself with you."

"Why are you telling me all this," Kitty said, "when you know that we spent a perfectly innocent afternoon?" She spoke too urgently and felt too shrill. Though she tried to submerge the feeling, Kitty realized that sometime, when she had the moral courage, she would have to confess to Rose that she and Mark had indeed found each other attractive that afternoon.

"I just want you to know," Rose said more calmly, "that it isn't all love and roses for anybody. And if Fred is good to you, if he cares for you as I think he does, you'd be a fool to leave him for greener pastures that turn out to be just as drab when you reach them."

"You sound like the voice of experience," Kitty said tenderly.

"I am," Rose answered. "That's why the boys are away at military school, you see. I didn't want them living here, where they could discover that their parents weren't . . . ."

"Rose."

"Oh, don't sound so dumbstruck, Kitty."

"But I always thought you two were the model of happiness."

Rose smiled with a gentle indulgence. "Yes. It's only civilized to keep one's dirty wash in the hamper, don't you think? And besides, Mark and I do care for each other. Only, we each have weaknesses that lead to separate paths now and then."

Kitty shivered from her fear to ask any questions. She had expected Rose to bolster her with the conventional strength of her good home and to find this instead, tumbling so readily from Rose's lips, shocked her. She realized just how unhappy Rose must be if, after all these years, she had finally broken down and confessed.

"It only goes to show," Kitty said, "how necessary it is for women to maintain an independence."

Kitty thought that she had spoken wisely, but Rose's derisive laugh implied that Kitty still had a lot to learn.

"Perhaps you ought to come with me to the hotel," Kitty said, "instead of my staying here with you."

"Oh, don't be silly," Rose answered crisply. "I wouldn't think of leaving Mark."

Kitty got up from the sofa and crossed to the liquor cabinet. There was much too much that didn't make sense. Too much and so close that Kitty felt herself breathing it in like poison gas.

"Do you want a drink?" she said, pouring herself a stiff one.

"All right," Rose said, acquiescing quietly.

"Good," Kitty laughed, trying to discover the snagged thread of her hopes and expectations. "We'll drink to the fact that we're women."

CHAPTER ELEVEN

This bit of knowledge from Rose made it doubly important to Kitty that she leave before Mark got home.

She felt that she could not face the two of them together. Nor did she want to see it, the facade of their happy home, the mockery of her beliefs and admiration.

If Rose and Mark were not happy together, who was?

But her legs felt unsteady. And Rose, from time to time, would take her hand and try to convince her not to worry.

"But I'm not worried," Kitty protested uneasily. "Why should I be worried when you have all your loose ends so remarkably under control?"

"Not worried about me, dear," Rose answered. "Worried for yourself. Come, admit it. Aren't you scared? You were never the kind to go out and do things for yourself, Kitty. Even as a little girl, you always liked to have company."

"That wasn't my fault," Kitty said, feeling that her lips were getting numb. "I was the baby in the family and nobody left me alone, that's why. It had nothing to do with what I wanted."

"True. But the results are the same."

"Are you trying to tell me, Rose, that you don't think I can stand on my own two feet?"

Rose set the glass carefully on a marble table top. "Of course you can," she said.

"You're humoring me."

"Why should I?"

"Because you still think I'm a child, that's why." Her eyelids were blinking too often. She could feel them beginning to burn and grow heavy. The whiskey hadn't been a good idea, after all. It was making her both sad and wild at the same time and she felt that her body was going to split right down the middle at any moment now.

"And I'm not a child," she went on. She felt like she could go on babbling forever.

"Of course you aren't."

The afternoon drifted silently by without Kitty's awareness. She knew only that Rose must have confidence. She had to convince her, make her admit and agree with her own fuzzy feelings.

It seemed that she had just gotten started on the mission of convincing Rose when the sound of Mark's car slid past the living room windows.

Kitty squinted at her watch.

"Yes, it's really eight o'clock," Rose said. "Now, let's all have a pleasant supper together and not mention too much of this to Mark."

"Not a word," Kitty agreed.

She went off to the bathroom as Mark came in the front door. She needed to comb her hair and fix her lipstick and sober up enough so that Mark wouldn't be able to see and surmise what had happened.

Cold water ran over her wrists and felt good. She wished she could be off in the mountains somewhere, far, far away from her guilt and the discomfort of facing Mark.

It was very real, this guilt, and not a figment of her imagination, Kitty told herself in the medicine cabinet mirror. Hadn't she found him attractive this past Sunday? Hadn't she therefore been a traitor to her sister, who loved her?

She wet a face towel and put it against her forehead. The world was so complicated and so dismal sometimes that she wondered why people bothered to go on. And yet, even in herself, she could feel the urge toward survival pressing strongly for command. She had gazed at life and found too much of it disgusting. But this didn't seem to matter. Her judgment was only a child's cry in the dark, something to hear and soothe, but not to accept as the final words about life and living.

Mark's voice filtered through the door and Rose's voice made a casual counterpoint as she was telling him about Kitty's visit.

Kitty smiled as she listened, wondering what excuse Rose would make up for her. But she realized after a while that Rose had neatly avoided this point. All excuses would be left in her own hands, to do with as she pleased.

She combed her hair once more, feeling loathe to leave the safety of the bathroom and stand up to Mark's sharp scrutiny. He was nobody's fool.

And when he saw that she was free, free as a sparrow, how would he act toward her then?

Kitty turned from the mirror, unable to face herself any longer. For if Mark decided to make advances toward her, she was not at all sure that she had the ability or the strength to fend him off.

Fred, Fred, she whispered hotly into the palm of her hand, *I hate you so for failing me.*

But when she stepped from the bathroom, Kitty moved with the calmness of a queen facing her troops on the brink of disaster. She realized that Mark would take his cue from her manner. If she gave him no hint of grief, and none of loneliness, he would leave her be. But if, for one single instant, she invited him to sympathize with her plight, to comfort her from the destructive storms of circumstance, then all would be lost.

"Well, how are you, Kitty? And how's the rug look?"

Mark's tone was distinctly ironic.

Already, Kitty thought. Already he's trying to discover what I'm doing here.

She sensed that Mark had begun to be suspicious, not because of her own manner, but because of Rose's.

Rose, who could keep up such a poised facade for the public, could never really intrigue with those close to her. The telltale lines of age around her mouth had deepened, as though she were forcibly restraining herself with an invisible lariat.

"The rug is just beautiful," Kitty replied, flouncing past him and picking up her glass, not quite empty of its third refill. "Shall I make you a Scotch and soda?"

"Great."

Mark eased himself onto the sofa, but far away from where Rose still sat.

As Kitty watched them from the side of her vision, she saw how acres of space seemed to exist here between them in the privacy of their own home. It seemed to her incredible that she had never noticed this before, when it was so obvious now.

Even the other night, when they had come to visit, Mark had been somehow different ... and Rose, too. She wondered if anything special had happened between them and how, but she didn't want to hear the details if it had.

She poured Scotch, remembering the proportions that Mark preferred, and gave him his glass.

They made an awkward threesome, Kitty felt .... Winken, Blinken and Stinken. But this was not the time to be crude, the way Fred could be crude smack in the middle of things, when it was important to be serious.

"You're looking good, Kitty," Mark said into his glass.

As the ice cubes rattled against each other, Kitty realized that she could not look Mark straight in the eyes. The sound of his voice seemed to be making fun of her hesitations. It was the same devilish kind of teasing he had used on her at the auction. Intimate and playful.

But now, in front of Rose, it humiliated her and Kitty felt like slapping Mark's face.

Rose said, "I still haven't shown you to your room, dear."

Anything to get away from Mark, Kitty thought, and she was relieved. She went with Rose down the foyer and up the wide stairs that glistened from faithful polishing.

"Where do you sleep?" Kitty said.

"Right next door to you," Rose smiled. "With Mark, if that's what you wanted to know."

Kitty wrinkled her nose in a little pout of annoyance, as though to say, How could you think such a thing? But it was exactly what she had wanted to know. It was like knowing the position of the lion's den, so that one could protect oneself....

A large tree brushed the tips of branches against the window panes in Kitty's room and she could smell the outdoors, the freshness of country, as she sat on the bed and watched Rose open closet doors and show her where things were.

It was obviously a boy's room, with simple but strong furniture, that seemed meant to be used rather than admired. A snapshot of Rose and Mark sitting in a rowboat protruded from a picture frame that held a man in football clothes.

"That's Junior's coach at school," Rose said, following her glance.

"And that's you and Mark in better days," Kitty added. But Rose had no reply.

It seemed to Kitty that maybe staying here, being company to her sister for a few days, would not be such a bad idea after all. They had drifted apart after marriage and now they might find each other again. Perhaps together....

Kitty cut short her own thoughts. It seemed too painful to consider being close friends with her sister, while at the same time she had such a yen for Mark. It was indecent somehow. Certainly disloyal. Even if she confessed her feelings to Rose, she would not feel absolved.

"If you need anything," Rose said, "just ask me. I don't know what we're going to do about clothes for you."

"I'll buy new ones," Kitty said blandly. "You know, it would give me a real pleasure to run up bills on the charge accounts Fred opened."

"Just to be spiteful?" Rose shook her head with a disapproving, but indulgent smile.

"No. To get some things that I like for a change."

"Well, come along. It's supper time and Mark will think we're making up secrets."

"You'll come shopping with me, Rose?"

"Of course."

By the time they arrived downstairs, the two were deeply involved in chatter of fashion and Kitty felt far more confident now of handling her feelings about Mark.

But when they were seated at the dinner table, just the three of them, a strange sensation began to prickle at Kitty's flesh. The empty chair beside her, where Fred would have been, made her feel somehow as though she had lost an arm.

"I hope," Kitty said with a hint in her voice, "that we're going to have some of that nice elderberry wine."

She didn't want to get drunk, but simply to keep a glow going like a small fire in the hearth, to warm her insides and cheer away the loneliness.

CHAPTER TWELVE

The three of them retired early and it wasn't until Kitty had taken off her shoes that she realized she could hear their voices coming through the wall.

At first she tried to ignore it. What Mark and Rose had to say to each other privately was none of her business. She slipped into one of Rose's nightgowns and snapped off the light. The room felt strange and eerie from the sound of the tree outside brushing its branches restlessly against the window.

She lay on her back and stared at the ceiling. She felt stiff all over, aching with fatigue, and yet she was unable to fall asleep. Her thoughts bounded to and fro, hammering against her skull. She wondered what Fred would be doing at this moment, then decided it was useless to think about him at all. The mattress, softer than hers at home, seemed to ball away beneath her back. She wished she had something to read that would divert her attention or a bedside radio to play. The boy's room held few of the trivial comforts to which she had become accustomed.

Alone in the dark and floating without roots, Kitty turned toward the sound of Mark's voice as she would have toward a beacon light.

She expected to hear only the usual chatter that proceeds between husband and wife. Or perhaps some mild bickering, since Rose had divulged that they weren't getting along too well.

But what she heard in Mark's voice surprised her and instinctively she pulled the covers up over her ears so that his words would not continue to penetrate her consciousness.

She had never heard Mark sounding amorous before. But the tone was unmistakable. A certain insinuating softness with meaningful silences that Kitty could easily fill in from her imagination.

Rose's responses came through just as clearly. Objections that began to fade as the moments passed.

"I want you tonight ...."

"Don't be silly, Mark."

"Silly?"

"Please! You're crowding me off the bed."

"Then don't run away."

"Mark, it's late."

"... never too late. Come on now, give a little. You know you love it ...."

Kitty shoved her head under the pillow. She could feel her nerves, her loneliness responding to the coaxing male voice. And she found herself wondering what it must be like to have Mark's hands ....

With a shudder, she pressed the pillow tighter over her head. And then, as silence descended, Kitty began to relax. It was perfectly normal for Mark and Rose to be doing what they were doing. Why should she feel embarrassed?

Gradually, she brought her head back into the air. She realized that she had been suffocating and that it wasn't, after all, her fault that their voices came through. She wasn't eavesdropping. She was just helpless to stop the sounds.

"... You're in good shape tonight, Rose. Nice and ..."

"Mark, don't be so rough."

"I thought you liked it that way. You were really a little lioness when we met."

"That was long ago."

"You haven't changed, Rose. Let me feel ...."

"Lower, darling. Just a little lower ...."

"Jelly roll."

"You're obscene."

"I could say worse."

"Ohhh, right there. Stay right there."

"Here, Rose. Touch me."

"You're solid as Gibraltar."

"What did you expect, noodles?"

"I always liked this best about you. You're such a big boy. God, sometimes I forget just how big ...."

"That's your fault. I could give it to you every night, if you wanted it."

"Sometimes I hate you too much to care."

"But not now."

"No, Mark. Not now."

"Well, don't strangle it to death, for chrissake ...."

Sick with fascination and her own desire, Kitty rolled across the mattress in agony. The vivid pictures forming across her brain displayed Mark in all his virility. She felt herself lying in Rose's place and her tingling skin began to perspire. Mark's mouth seemed to travel over her body, his urgency to press down on her ....

Desperately, she flung herself from the bed and tiptoed down the stairs to the darkened living room. Putting on a single lamp, she searched out the bottle of Scotch and filled a glass half full. She would stay down here all night if necessary. Sleep on the couch. Anything to escape what she had heard and what she wanted so terribly for herself.

Opening a window, she stood still in the cold night air, but she could hardly feel it against her burning flesh. Her body had gone numb. She could barely see or think straight and, though she wanted to get drunk, even the whiskey did not seem to reach her.

Kitty hugged herself close within the circle of her own arms, as though to protect herself from the waves of loneliness closing in on her. This was the first time in many years she had spent a night without Fred and a great, gaping hole yawned in her heart where once there had been love.

She stared up at the stars with yearning eyes and the sky seemed to film over and the stars blurred.

But there was no one to see her unhappiness now. No one to help her and very probably, no one who might even want to. Kitty realized that only she could help herself.... that she must stand on her own feet and cry on her own shoulder.

An hour passed with these whirling and unaccustomed thoughts. She tried to get comfortable on the couch, but it was too narrow. And sleep was a long way off under the best of circumstances. Going back to the stairs, she wondered if it were safe to go back to bed yet. Well, there was nothing more that she could hear. She had managed somehow to live through the worst of it, so she might as well return.

She climbed the smooth steps, feeling a small pain in the pit of her stomach roll back and forth as though it were lying in a hammock. It was the sickness of desire unfulfilled and it had left her breasts hard and heavy, yet tender. Her throat ached from the strain of holding back all the nervous responses and her temples ached.

It's been some night, Kitty thought ... and managed to laugh at her predicament.

At the top of the stairs she felt an urgent impulse to run quickly past their room with her hands pressed over her ears. Then she took a deep breath and forced herself to walk calmly by, as though nothing had happened.

Back in her own room, she could not suppress the urge to listen.

Nothing.

Then, a faint snore.

So it was over.

She could just see them, lying side by side, each released now from the animal urge that had brought them together.

Yes, marriage was a convenience sometimes, Kitty told herself. If nothing else, it solved the problem of going out on rainy nights ....

She sat down on Junior's desk chair and put her chin on her palms, seeing nothing in her future but an endless chain of rainy nights ... and loneliness.

CHAPTER THIRTEEN

She slept fitfully and by morning, the alcohol had turned sour in her stomach and darkened her future with a brown haze. Mark banged out of the bedroom and into the bath with a kind of chipper enthusiasm that Kitty wished she felt for herself.

Slowly, she dressed in her room, hoping that Mark would take a quick breakfast and leave before she would have to see him. She had hardly finished putting on her make-up when Rose's knock startled her from the cage of her thoughts.

"Did you have a good night?" Rose said, one hand in the pocket of a long dressing gown.

Kitty studied the masses of silver hair combed out around her sister's shoulders. It was beautiful hair and this morning it framed a beautiful, calm face.

"Yes," Kitty lied easily.

"We're having Canadian bacon this morning." Rose examined one cuticle and pulled off a minute hangnail. "It's Mark's favorite."

"After all you told me, yesterday, Rose, I didn't expect you to be so full of joy this morning," Kitty ventured.

"Whims come and go," Rose said. "One has to be flexible."

Kitty's mouth quivered into a bitter smile. "If I were that flexible, I'd be dead."

"You'd probably be home enjoying life a little," Rose corrected briskly.

"You've always been the optimist," Kitty said, tightening the belt of her dress. "And the stubborn one."

Rose didn't answer her. She only smiled with a secret, beautiful knowledge that Kitty understood, but didn't dare reveal that she knew. After all, she had often been trapped into forgetting in Fred's arms, just as Rose had been trapped in Mark's. But a brief moment of passion could not change the facts of everyday life. Not for either of them.

"I hope you go back to Fred," Rose said after a while.

And Kitty tossed her head with determination. "I never will."

The aroma of fresh, crisp bacon drifted upstairs, reminding Kitty that the world was spinning by without her. She felt that if she didn't make a move soon, it might spin away and lose her forever. She went arm in arm down the stairs with Rose, privately deciding that this afternoon she would go quietly on her way to a hotel. It was no good living like this, three in a house. No matter how many rooms there were, even if she slept in the basement and heard nothing more than the boiler thundering on and off, she knew that she would be an intruder. And a dangerous one, perhaps. The tingling of desire in her belly had refused to leave. She felt her brittle nerves threatening to break into bits. If she didn't get out of here soon, she might well lose control and do something she'd regret for the rest of her days.

"Morning, Kit Kat," Mark greeted her while he spread thick sweeps of butter across dark toast.

He had showered and shaved and all of him glistened. The tips of his glasses' frames, sticking from a jacket pocket, caught a sliver of morning light and reflected it back to Kitty. Ignoring the affectionate term he had used, she sat down unobtrusively and reached to the buffet for a glass of juice.

Rose, standing before the spread of closed tureens, lifted lids and scooped portions of scrambled eggs onto plates.

"None for me, thanks," Kitty said.

Mark glanced at her. "Breakfast is the most important meal of the day," he said, half serious, half lightheartedly. "It picks up depleted energies."

Kitty felt her cheeks going warm from the meaning beneath his words. She dared not look at him now and reveal that she understood his allusion, which, she felt sure, had been meant for Rose alone.

Or maybe not.

Mark cleared his throat and stirred sugar into his cup. "Now, Kitty, don't tell me you aren't hungry for anything."

She felt trapped. If she spoke, he would know. And if she did not, he would suspect.

"Yes, I believe I'll have a little of those eggs," she said, directing her remark purposefully at Rose.

Then Kitty saw that she had blundered completely. For Rose glanced at her with suspicion tucked neatly into the pinching corners of her nostrils. Her eyes said, Why are you being rude to him?

So it was hopeless.

Kitty shut her eyes for an instant and sighed. There wasn't a thing she could do about it.

Except leave.

And she had every intention of doing exactly that. She would be leaving a mess behind and Rose would never again trust her completely. But it seemed lately that no matter what she did, there was always some sort of mess afterward. Like a Typhoid Mary, Kitty felt herself stumbling blindly across the earth, spreading unhappiness and complication.

Doggedly, she ate her eggs and drank some black coffee, needing it to give her a lift and to dilute the residue of alcohol in her veins. The sleepless night had left her rocky and careless. She wanted only to get away from everyone and everything, perhaps start all over again like a newborn chick.

She could sense that Mark was in no hurry to leave. Time dragged on past nine o'clock. Wasn't he going to the office at all today? His presence constricted her. Everytime she glanced at him, she could hear his voice saying those things to Rose, could almost feel his hands. ...

"It's a beautiful morning," Kitty said, getting up from the table. "I think I'll go for a walk."

"That would be nice," Rose said.

Her tone revealed to Kitty that even this morning, Rose wanted to be alone with her husband.

The afterplay of love. She understood it clearly, knew how the body stretched out its needing languorously over long waves of time.

Almost running, Kitty got to the front door and flung herself into the open air.

Early spring blossomed all around her as though everything in the universe was glad to be alive. Bright, crisp greens stood illuminated by the brilliant blue above and the tree that had frightened her last night sang this morning with the songs of hidden birds.

Kitty stumbled down the street, going no place and yet going everywhere, needing to drink an infusion of life and gulp down the sun's bright energy. Her arms trembled to reach out and wrap themselves around things, anything, just for the sheer pleasure of contact with beauty and happiness.

And with this feeling came back the recognition that she was alone. Utterly, irrevocably alone.

Yet she knew, as she walked down the lonely street, that she had been meant to share things. Pleasure was only half a joy without someone beside her to respond with her.

She turned right around then and went straight back to the garage and into her car, backing onto the street with a squeal and driving off before she had a chance to blunder again with Rose.

She hoped sincerely that someday Rose would understand and forgive her. She would telephone from the city and explain how she had been overwhelmed by the need to start arranging her life. With tact, perhaps, she could avoid the whole problem of Mark and his threat to her body.

Yet whether or not Rose would accept her explanations was very much beside the point. She knew only that she had to get away from Mark before she made a fool of herself. And she knew that she had to find someone of her own again. Someone to take Fred's place in her heart and in her arms.

She had promised herself the luxury of a hotel room and when she reached the city, she thumbed through the yellow pages, wondering which to choose from among so many.

At random, she settled on one with air conditioning and television in every room; it had an East Side address, not too far from Madison Avenue.

She phoned, made a reservation, then went on a shopping spree. If she were going to live in one of the better places, she would have to dress and act like one of the better class women.

The purchasing went smoothly. Everything she saw, she wanted and what she could not carry in the trunk of the car, she had forwarded to the hotel.

When she was alone in the hotel room, she tumbled her packages onto the bed and fell down beside them, stretching and humming to herself, exuberant with expectations. Then she rolled onto her belly and picked up the phone.

Dirk Thornwald answered the ring with a preoccupied voice. Kitty could just see him, with the phone in one hand and the stethoscope in the other.

He was too busy this afternoon. But would she be available this evening?

Yes, this evening would be perfect, Kitty said, encouraged that he was taking the aggressive role out of her hands.

A warm feeling of satisfaction flooded through her. Dirk Thornwald didn't know it yet, but he was going to introduce her to a whole new circle of friends.... professional men, who had both money and prestige.

Kitty rolled over onto her back, kicked one leg and thought about her new future. Things were bound to improve, now that she had cut herself off completely from Fred.

And she intended to have all the fun she had missed during the lean and drab years of being a housewife.

CHAPTER FOURTEEN

Dirk arrived precisely on time, as Kitty had known he would.

"Good evening, Dirk," she said, waiting with suppressed animation while he surveyed the scenery of her figure.

"Well, Kitty," he said at last. "Just what did you have in mind?"

She knew that if she told him the blunt truth, he would fall over backward from the shock.

"I'll leave that up to you," she answered instead, flirting with him ever so mildly as she moved away from the door and invited him in with lowered eyes.

"You remind me of a whirlwind," he said, his glance roving the single bedded room with its table tops cluttered by the smaller purchases of jewelry and cosmetics. "We've known each other three days and already you've moved out of your house, set yourself up in a new residence and are in, I take it, the process of divorcing your husband."

"Is that bad?" Kitty said. "I thought it was one Dr. Thornwald who prescribed that I find something to do with myself."

"Something constructive is what I had in mind, my dear," Dirk said gently.

Kitty sensed something elusive about him tonight that she did not quite enjoy. His manner seemed a trifle too flip, his approach to her insultingly casual. She wondered where the respect had gone, that slight attitude of deference she had liked so much at their first meeting back at the house.

"One can't begin to build without first destroying the old roots," Kitty said, trying hard for dignity.

A twinge of disappointment flickered through her. She could not imagine why the new sapphire dress did not overwhelm him. His one brief gaze had sized her up and, it seemed, filed her away for future reference. This was not the response she had counted on and she meant to do something about it before the evening was out.

"Destroying old roots is fine," Dirk said, taking the cigarette she offered him. "It's the ways and means that are open to discussion."

She handed over the book of matches and waited for him to strike a light.

"I take it, then, you don't approve?" she said, trying to make a farce of his seriousness.

"No comment."

"Does that mean that you have no opinion or are you simply being diplomatic?" As she spoke, she sauntered about the room, showing him every angle of her figure, displaying herself like a precious jewel that he should be greedy to possess.

Dirk smiled and dropped the match into a glass ash tray. "I don't know how to be diplomatic," he said. "At least, not sufficiently to the satisfaction of the fairer sex."

"Oh, I doubt that," Kitty smiled. "Seems to me you do pretty well at whatever interests you."

Kitty watched her attempt to flatter his ego fall flat. It lay at her feet like a dead thing that she wished she could have destroyed before it was born.

Stalling for time, she tried to get the feel of him. What would make him flush with pleasure? But each of her attempts seemed childish and rang hollow with insincerity. With Fred, it had been simple. In fact, she could keep Fred happy while she was thinking about what to serve for the next day's dinner.

But this one, this quicksilver man, posed a problem. He smoked his cigarette and answered her questions. He agreed with her unexpectedly and disagreed when it was most embarrassing. Kitty began to feel like a disembodied spirit. Maybe he was a woman hater. He must be something strange, she decided as he helped her on with her evening wrap, if he didn't respond to the basic calls of nature.

Nature or sex?

Kitty realized as they rode down in the elevator that she had been tingling all day like a charged wire. Her personal frustrations might be exaggerating matters.

Dirk Thornwald was probably the slow type. When a man deals with matters of life and death, she supposed that he learned not to jump hastily into anything.

Consoling herself thus, she climbed into the taxi he had hailed and sat deliberately at the far side of the seat from him. She didn't care where they were going or what he had planned. Only one thing interested her this night ... and she would make Dirk beg for it, when he finally got around to asking.

"I didn't have a chance to order the paint yet," Kitty said to show him that she could still think about practical matters.

"That doesn't surprise me," he smiled. "I expected to do it myself, anyhow. Probably tomorrow and I have someone to do the work, too, so you don't have to concern yourself any further."

Kitty smiled grimly. "I'm sure you can hardly wait to move in," she said.

Dirk grinned widely. "I'm every bit as anxious as you were to move out."

Huffily, Kitty stared out the window, wondering how to get even with him, how to find his weak spots and make them more tender.

"Well, what are we doing here?" Kitty blurted as the cab pulled up in front of Dirk's office.

"You'll see," he said, paying the cabbie and climbing out after her.

Determined not to seem overly curious, she went with him into the darkened office, following the trail of lamp light as they moved from room to room.

Pausing in the consultation room, Dirk said, "Sit down, Kitty." From a narrow cabinet that divided the bookcases, he took out glasses and a tall bottle of yellow liquid that Kitty had never seen before.

"We'll have a pleasant evening at home," Dirk said blandly. "Just the two of us."

Kitty sat uncomfortably poised on the edge of her chair. She could not imagine what Dirk felt toward her and how to get the situation back under her own control.

That was the most irritating thing about Dirk Thornwald, Kitty realized as she accepted the drink he offered and tasted it with little sips. He always managed to put her at a loss, make her feel like a child just learning to walk. This attitude humiliated her. At least, she wanted to think so. But a secret twinge of pleasure contradicted this.

"This is good," she said, looking into the glass.

"Good and strong," Dirk said. He was sitting on the edge of his desk and swinging one leg. "Tell me, Kitty, have you and Fred settled this separation amicably?"

Kitty squirmed with discomfort. "Why bring up unpleasant subjects?"

"It's in your best interests to tell me, Kitty. Otherwise, if I send the monthly rent check to him, you won't see any part of it. And obviously, you could use the money."

Kitty, suddenly realizing her financial predicament, forgot to be indignant at Dirk's prying.

She sat back and arranged on her face the little smile that would cover up the fact that she was thinking.

Certainly, she had no grounds on which to leave Fred. He had been as faithful as a Saint Bernard all the years of their marriage. And if she left him, he wasn't required by law to make any financial provision for her.

"Besides," Dirk interrupted her thoughts, "if he should get mad enough and decide to sell, that'll really leave you up the creek."

"Yes," she murmured. "I tell you what. Just pay the rent to me every month and that'll settle everything."

Dirk burst out laughing. "Wouldn't it, though?" His eyes twinkled with appreciation for her blunt solution. "Too bad the lease doesn't have your name on it."

Kitty remembered angrily how she had told Fred that she wanted no part of renting out their home ... and now it was coming true in a way too ironic to take calmly.

"I would suggest, my little friend," Dirk refilled his glass, "that either you go back to where the bread and butter is or discover, quite conveniently and with legal proof, that your husband is being unfaithful to you."

"Impossible," Kitty mumbled grumpily to herself. "I'll get a Mexican divorce and the heck with him."

"That still leaves you on the losing end, unless you make some kind of arrangement with him."

Kitty, who had eaten very little all day, felt a sudden drop as though her insides were caving in. She wanted to stand up and walk off the drink, but her legs felt flimsy as paper and she couldn't find the energy to lift herself from the chair.

Dirk came over to her. "Having trouble?"

"It's nothing." She rested back again. "Too much drinking and not enough of anything else."

"Except nervous excitement."

His sympathetic voice, a sudden change from the careless attitude, relieved Kitty of a heavy burden.

"I really thought," she said, "that you didn't like me, Dirk." She did not look at him.

"There are some things about you that I don't like," he said frankly. "But that's not the whole picture. Lost little girls appeal to me anyway."

She couldn't tell whether he was being serious or trying to chide her out of the mood of hopelessness beginning to creep up.

"Perhaps," she said from a deep well of desperation, "if I have no reason to divorce Fred, he can find one to divorce me."

She tilted her head up, inviting Dirk to take her and to be kind.

"Is that the way it is?" he muttered.

Kitty reached out and trailed her fingertips over his mouth. "You've diagnosed the patient, doctor," she whispered. "Now, cure her."

He leaned over and brought her quickly up to his mouth.

The taste of him, so cool, so contained, felt to Kitty like an oasis in the middle of her scorching troubles. Her body shuddered with rising delirium as she sensed the newness of a strange body against her own.

Where Fred had been hard and thick, Dirk was lean and supple. He seemed to wind around her like a charmed snake.

Kitty abandoned herself to the sensations. His smooth cheek with its long jawline skimmed down along her neck and to the hollow of her throat. Deep inside, Kitty smiled with a private satisfaction. There were some things that women controlled, and not men ... and passion was one of them.

He stood her up, holding her like a doll tightly around her waist. His enormous strength pressed her hard and squeezed her breathless for an instant. Then he brought her to the leather couch and sat her down beside him.

"You've been drinking a great deal, haven't you?" he said.

"Do you have to be professional just now?" Kitty said with light amusement.

She was unfastening the top buttons of her dress, opening the neckline low enough to reveal the first swell of her breasts, but no further. She wanted the satisfaction of Dirk reaching for her, needing her, and she sat back from him so that he would have to stretch to touch her.

He turned around and put his head into her lap, swinging his legs over the arm of the couch.

"Comfortable?"

"Yes, very," Dirk smiled. He reached one hand to the curve of her breast. "Are you?"

She bent over and kissed him on one closed eyelid. "I'll do," she murmured.

This was no position for a man to be aggressive, Kitty felt with a slight impatience. What the hell was he waiting for? Her body, aroused, demanded attention. Her thighs quivered beneath his head and her belly pulsed, threatening again the pain she had suffered after last night's dismal strain.

"You've never been serious about a woman," Kitty said, trying to cover up her nervousness.

"What makes you say that?"

She shrugged. "Intuition."

He began to sit up, keeping his hands on her all the while. "Would you like me to be serious about you, Kitty?"

She detected in the question a certain chiding, as though Dirk could feel free to play with her, but not to trust her.

"Don't strain yourself," she said with a touch of acid.

"Oh, it's a pleasure, believe me."

"I believe you," she answered, wondering why Fate had meant for her to be a man's plaything.

But again, her body denied the importance of all the questions buzzing through her brain. Her flesh tingled with the need to be caressed and she wished that Dirk would move to take her clothes off.

Somehow, in the stark professional surroundings, it seemed wrong for her to display the greed of her passion. Wrong, yet natural, for nature could not be denied and demanded both respect and satiety.

Beyond the Venetian blinds, she heard the passage of street traffic. It seemed to her that anyone could bend down and look in, if they knew what was going on in here.

"Are we quite safe?" she asked tentatively.

"From what?" Dirk smiled, feeling down along her breasts.

"Curious eyes."

"Of course," he laughed. "Did you think I wanted a picture of us in the morning papers?"

Kitty laughed at herself too and relaxed. She could put herself into Dirk's care and depend on his prudence for protection.

As his touch probed and discovered all the little desires that beat inside her with feathery wings, Kitty abandoned all attempt at discretion.

With an overwhelming need, she flung her arms around his neck and pulled him tight, pressing her breasts to him, flattening her belly against his and squirming her hips along him to urge the rise of his desire.

"Oh, God, how I need it," she whispered and her body felt like a typhoon rolling quickly toward its own destruction.

She grasped his hands and made them move faster to find her nakedness, then pressed his palm hard against her.

The dam inside her burst and her craving spilled over. She could not wait for him to undress her or to take off his own clothing. It must be now, instantly. She had to feel the surging pressure of him, to relieve the desire that felt like a hungry giant in her belly.

Struggling to find him, her fingers touched his maleness and guided him to her.

"Be good to me," she pleaded. "I need it so badly."

She heard his answering grunt and then felt the straightening pressure of him, forcing wide her hips.

Lifting herself, her whole body seemed to cling and grasp. Her mouth lolled open. The mass of her blonde hair tangled round her face. Her long fingernails scratched down his back, clawing into his soft jacket.

It happened almost instantly for her, exploding in waves that grew wider and wider … that consumed and drowned her. Then cooled, leaving her to lie on her back, half smiling and limp.

She felt like one who had been washed up from a great ocean and miraculously saved.

CHAPTER FIFTEEN

But Kitty could not hide from the truth forever.

She could feel it beginning to shine its light through the darkness, while Dirk, who had gotten up so that she could stretch out at her ease, poured more of the yellow liquid and drank it down.

"Take off your things," he said quietly, "and make yourself comfortable."

Now that it was over and her senses returning, Kitty found it difficult to face him. She had felt no love, after all. She had felt nothing at all for Dirk, only the sheer necessity of desire. Dirk was the aspirin she had taken for her headache and she wished that she could lock him back in the closet until the next time … if there were a next time.

"You were right, weren't you?" she said. "About Fred, I mean."

He offered her a glass, but she shook her head no. There were too many things to be done and she could not afford to float in limbo forever.

"So what are you going to do about it?" Dirk said.

Kitty lifted one leg and eyed the snags in her stockings. She could sense that she was a mess. Her appearance reflected how she felt and she wished that Dirk would have the decency to be affectionate so she could forget how they had both used each other. For he, obviously, felt no more for her than she had felt for him.

"I'll have to see him eventually," Kitty said, talking about Fred, but unable to feel any closeness to her words. Fred was like a balloon that had floated off into the sky and become a mere speck that she was squinting up at in the glare.

"And when you do see him?"

"I don't know," Kitty admitted. "I just don't know."

Vaguely, she remembered that Dirk was going to be her stepping stone. That through him she had planned to meet others and take her choice of any eligible bachelor with lots of money. She had intended to get married again … to be kept, anything that would keep her going until she could straighten out the tattered shreds of her life.

But looking at Dirk, she realized that giving in to her sexual needs had been the wrong answer. If he introduced her to anyone, she could be sure that her reputation would have proceeded her.

You don't get a husband by being a whore.

Unless you happen to be an extraordinarily good one.

Kitty studied her nailpolish with deep intent.

"Dirk," she said, "tell me about you." Her voice, languid and coaxing, meant to discover her own potential. "Was it good?"

"Sure, honey," he said carelessly. "And I'll be back for more, real soon."

His nonchalance irritated her. By tomorrow morning, would he even remember her name?

Men were flexible. They took it when they could get it.

Kitty understood that any woman on Dirk's couch could have made him respond. There was no trick to that, surely. And she realized now that she had stopped too soon. She had let sex become a bauble, to be used once and then tossed away.

She must go further than that with Dirk. Watching his cool, easy motions, she realized how necessary it was to reach out to him. Make him respond, not only with his body, but with the completeness of his being. Make him give passion and intimacy … but reveal, too, the personality beneath that she did not really comprehend.

"Dirk, come here and sit down with me, will you?" Her voice, an open invitation, made him cock his head with curiosity.

"Did I forget something?" he smiled.

She caught the obscene meaning behind the words and shuddered. He would probably never believe that she might want something from him beyond the use of his body.

"Yes," she smiled back.

He came to the couch and she reached her warm fingers around to the back of his neck, stroking lightly where the soft hairs shaved away into smoothness.

Dirk neither moved toward her nor pulled away. She could feel him waiting, alert yet still calm, for her to reveal the workings behind her attempt at affection.

"You may not realize this," she began softly, "but you know my whole life history, but for all I know, you might be a married man with ten children."

Her opening was harmless enough, she saw, as Dirk's mouth relaxed into a wide grin.

Kitty ran the tips of her fingers over the smile, tracing the outlines of the smooth face and beginning to find it pleasant.

"So you want to know about me," Dirk said and he swung around just enough to slide his hands up along her breasts and cup their weight. "There isn't much to tell."

Kitty could feel sensation beginning to stir through her body again. She had not planned on that. She had meant to stay in control, to be the perfect courtesan who could heat men till they burned and stay cold herself.

"Well, let's see," she said, trying to keep her voice from trembling. "Do you have a middle name?"

Dirk put his lips to her throat. "The vital statistics, if you must know," he said with clinical conciseness, "are as follows. Born at home, in November. The last of four sons ...."

He was making fun of her, Kitty knew. Perhaps Dirk was one of those people who were successful because nothing human could touch them? Yet this seemed impossible. The way he handled her body, he had to feel something.

Already she felt his need rise, reminding her that there were other needs more immediate than her clumsy approach to the secret of Dirk's character.

Her fingers strayed to the buttons of her blouse. They worked slowly, but surely; and while her thoughts drifted, she slipped out of her blouse. With a slow, practiced gesture she undid her bra.

Leaning back against the couch, feeling him search and probe along her, the desire to talk seemed to drift off to a never-never land where people understood each other instantly, through magic or chemical sympathy.

Kitty closed her eyes and sighed.

She felt his sure hands unzip her skirt along the side of her hip and she arched while he pulled the skirt and slip over her hips.

"I wish you really liked me," she murmured, watching him gaze at her nakedness.

"But I do," Dirk whispered against her belly. "Can't you tell?"

Kitty put her palm on the back of his head and felt the soft strands of his hair. "I mean really," she said, "as a person."

She could sense him hesitating.

"People who don't depend on each other too much," he said at last, "usually wind up being better friends."

To Kitty, it was a cryptic remark. Had she ever depended upon anyone except Fred? Did she want to depend upon Dirk?

"I don't know what you mean," she answered, lifting her hips slightly to give his hand room to move behind her buttocks.

"No, you wouldn't," Dirk said. "But you see, many women have a way of mistaking dependency for love. They find a man who can satisfy them, soothe and comfort them ... make it quite unnecessary for them to think. And then, when they've reached a state of glazed eyes, they call it love and expect marriage."

Kitty felt her stomach tightening in protest. But just as suddenly, she relaxed. What he said didn't apply to her, after all. It must be what had happened to him long ago.

"Is that the kind of woman you got involved with?" she said, testing.

"Only once," Dirk replied.

"And for you, once of anything is enough," Kitty said.

"Not quite."

His hands, moving down along her buttocks, raised her gently.

Kitty's widening body abandoned itself to his touch and his manipulations. No matter what else she might think of him, Dirk could make her respond in a way that erased all past and all future. She knew that later she would be sorry for this. He had a way of making her seem like a fool. And at the same time, his careful excitation of her senses made Kitty feel like a queen.

She brought him into the circle of her legs and poised him above her. There was something about the shape of his body that made all of his movements precise without being brisk. Easily, Kitty could understand how a woman could come to depend on him.

"Did you love her?" Kitty muttered, wanting selfishly to blend into this other woman on whom Dirk had spent time and trouble.

"Yes," Dirk answered.

The pressure of his lips on hers stopped all further question. She could do nothing but press back against the body that insisted and forced her into the pillows. His wide shoulders curved round her so that his body felt like a cave obstructing all view of the world outside.

Her breasts, hard against him, tingled. Pearls of perspiration slid down her sides. She felt herself melting into a pool that welled upward from her knees, lapped gently through her belly and spread along her arms.

Clinging to him, the burning in her gave off great waves of heat that undulated and created a haze. Beyond it, she could feel Dirk's urgency beating in tempo with her own.

"Hurry," she muttered.

Her body half slid from the couch as he pressed relentlessly. Her temples throbbed as her head fell backward.

Vaguely she felt Dirk's arm moving to brace her fall and they slid gently to the carpet.

Kitty spread her legs wide. The nap of the rug itched lightly on her naked back, yet she wanted it this way. One could get no lower than doing this sort of thing on the floor with a strange man. A man who, she knew, had closed his heart to love. A man who obviously believed in ethical standards for his profession and a cool aloofness from his sex life.

"Are your brothers nice?" she said as he moved inside her, wanting to be spiteful, to hit out at this man whom she could never really touch.

"If you like married businessmen," he answered, taunting her. "With children."

He rolled her onto her side and then over, so that she was sitting on top of him.

The sudden act surprised Kitty and the movement of her pelvis stopped in momentary puzzlement.

"It's all right," Dirk smiled, balancing her and steadying her with a hand on either hip. "Since you like being in the driver's seat, I thought I'd give it to you."

Kitty flushed. She had been too nosy.

"I...just wanted to...understand you a little," she said honestly.

"The hell you do!"

He did not seem angry, merely suavely evasive. But it was too late for secrets, Kitty felt with a sly satisfaction. She could piece him together now. How he had grown up, struggling probably at school, cajoled by brothers who thought of money first, last and always.

It was easy enough to understand why Dirk was so aloof. No doubt it was his way of protecting himself from the spearheads that had hurt so sharply at first.

And adding to this a disappointment in first love, Kitty could not really blame him for lack of confidence in the female sex.

She could simply hope that Dirk would learn, as she was learning, that one could not really live alone and like it.

These thoughts wafted in semi-vagueness through her head as her body responded to a greater, more immediate clarity.

Lying down flat on top of him, she put her face along the high tendons of his neck. The tip of her tongue touched his skin and tasted salt.

Her arms slid beneath his shoulders and clung. If they could only just start again, from the beginning, maybe they could learn to know each other and to trust.

"Dirk ... Dirk, be kind to me," she whispered. "And I'll try to be good for you, I really will."

"Is that a fact?"

His laughter was like broken glass, hard and cutting.

There was no denying her foolishness.

And no denying his cruelty.

If she had had the strength, Kitty would have gotten up that instant and run from him. But she couldn't stop herself. Not now. It was too late ....

Shimmying her hips, she centered herself more perfectly on him and gave herself to the galloping lust that did not give a good damn what she thought of Dirk or of herself.

Her body would always master her, Kitty sensed. A hot flush of shame mingled with her desire, speeding it on, wanting her to hurry and get it all over with.

When it finally happened, her body tightened with convulsive rage that drew satisfaction and continued to draw it till she had drawn both herself and Dirk completely dry.

Rolling away from him, she put her face to the carpet, needing to rest and regain energy for leaving him.

Kitty touched her dry lips with a cracked tongue. She might be able to walk out of here, but she would never be able to forget this night.

If nothing else, it had taught her a lesson. She might be greedy for sex or greedy for life, but she would never demand more from a man than he could give.

And Dirk could give her nothing of the human needs, of love, of gentle kindness, of that intimate trust she had known with Fred.

Hastily now, she got up and pulled on her clothes.

"You'd better take me back to the hotel," she said abruptly. "I want to go home."

He looked at her with question.

"I said, take me home, Dirk."

Dirk lifted his still full glass. "Don't you want to comb your hair first?"

Her cheeks burst into flames that licked upward to the roots of her hair. She deserved to be treated like trash ....

"The bathroom's that way," he tilted his head to a direction behind him.

Kitty fled toward the refuge of privacy.

She closed the door and stood over the sink, letting icy water run hard and splash against the shallow curve of porcelain. The small mirror above the sink stared at her with merciless eyes, revealing her bleary, swollen face and the dishevelled mess of her clothing.

Kitty hadn't even imagined that it would be this bad and she ducked her head quickly from the sight of herself, splashing the cold water over her face till she shivered.

Enough is enough.

To start all over again she would need anonymity. Be where no one knew either her past or her future. She didn't even want

Dirk to take her home now. Facing him was too painful to make it worth it.

But she had to be sensible. At least she had to try. For where was there to go?

Not to Fred. She couldn't stand the thought of being choked off again from all hope.

Not to Rose, surely, with Mark hanging around like a lecherous pussy cat.

And Dirk? Dirk's contemptuous eyes would ruin any chance she could arrange for meeting the proper men.

Kitty took a lipstick from her purse and opened her compact. She would have to do it all alone, just as she had realized earlier in the day. She would have to climb every inch under her own steam. Slowly, she rebuilt her make-up job and told herself in an encouraging whisper that a good night's sleep would restore her looks and bolster her confidence.

When she came out of the bathroom, Kitty walked with more erect posture and slower, smoother steps.

"Now, that's better," Dirk said, smiling kindly.

Kitty saw the smile, but she didn't believe in its sincerity. Doctors, after all, had a reputation. She should have remembered that in the very beginning.

"Come on," he said. "I'll take you for a bite to eat and that'll round out the evening."

"No," Kitty said firmly. "Just take me home."

She felt his eyes studying her hard, relentlessly, as though he were searching her for some dread disease.

"I mean it, Dirk," she said to reinforce her own conviction. "You see, I learn from my mistakes."

Dirk lit a cigarette and handed it to her. "All right," he said. "If that's what you want."

It was only a few short blocks from his office to her hotel and Kitty felt that she wanted to walk. She needed the fresh air to blow the sex from her body and she needed the feel of people all around her to remind her that she wasn't alone, really ... that all she had to do was be accessible and she would find friends waiting at every turn.

"No, don't come in with me," Kitty said at the entrance to the lobby.

"Discretion?" Dirk smiled.

"Better late than never."

"You're a funny girl, Kitty. I hope you learn someday how to make yourself content."

"So do I," she said, letting him take her hand for a moment.

"Well, if you ever need anything, if there's ever any way I can be of help ..."

Kitty listened to his offer, but the words seemed to hit against her eardrums and bounce off. She had trusted Dirk too soon and now she hated herself for it.

"I'm not drowning yet," she said with a pleasant, covering smile.

"Of course you aren't."

But when Kitty left him and crossed the lobby all by herself to the elevator, she wondered just how long she would float on these whimsical waves of bravado.

Alone in her room, she slipped a quarter into the pay television and turned channels until she reached something loud and laughy.

She peeled off her rumpled dress and let it lay where it fell, glad to be free of the slimy thing, as though she were shedding last year's skin. The dress held memories for her now, recollections of failure, and she couldn't look at it. She called room service and told the porter to give the dress to whichever chambermaid it might fit.

Then she went into the adjoining bathroom and soaked her body in water as hot as it would stand. A dreaminess began to slide up over her. Despite her treacherous position, she would have to get some sleep and just let everything else go hang until morning.

Maybe tomorrow, it would all come clean and bright ... maybe tomorrow.

But Kitty didn't sleep a wink.

She sat up, thinking that it must be morning, only to discover that the sky was still dark. Fast, high riding clouds covered a three-quarter moon with gauzy veils. A night for headless horsemen, she thought, and lit a cigarette to hasten the minutes till dawn.

The empty bed seemed to her preposterously small, as though her life had been torn in half. Premonitions of living alone frightened her. Now she wished she had a child, something to cuddle, something to caress, something to devote her life and her love to without fear of being used.

Footsteps in the hallway told Kitty of other people coming back at this late hour. And of people leaving, too.

Where did people go, she wondered, at three o'clock in the morning.

Someplace.

Anyplace would be better than this silent room that seemed to echo with her own emptiness.

Kitty put on a clean dress, something pale blue and reminiscent of an evening sky. Clothes had so often made her feel good. But tonight, they seemed so lifeless, so bereft of good suggestions that she wondered if they really were the same ones she had chosen earlier with such delight and expectation.

The bloat had gone out of her eyelids and only tension lines told of her unhappiness.

Make-up would cover them.

When she had finished dressing, Kitty decided that the best approach would be simply to put one foot in front of the other and go wherever her steps would lead.

The lobby, huge and rather empty, was a pale pink glow from lamp shades. She gave her key to the desk clerk who was checking a book of accounts and not at all interested in Kitty or her problems.

She wandered, then, back into the streets, broad and rather pretty, she thought, in this lull between crowds. The shops with their awnings rolled up seemed to her like people, staring out at the world with vacant eyes.

But there were no signs of human life. And there would be none for many hours.

Then where?

She strolled at random, moving toward Fifth Avenue and the great circle at Fifty Ninth Street.

Late comers in dinner jackets, women in evening gowns floated past uniformed doormen. People glittered and laughed with a carefree animation.

She felt certain that she would find something here, if she would only look. This was the crossroads of the high class world and finding someone would be simply a matter of time and the right combination of circumstances.

But as minutes passed and she found herself loitering in front of the darkened windows of an antique shop, irritation began again. Was she a common street-walker?

Never. Never. She would die first, Kitty told herself, while her glance rolled hungrily over every passing man.

CHAPTER SIXTEEN

B y dawn, Kitty had wandered far from the hotel and the high class hopes with which she had started out.

Her feet burned from walking so many miles of pavement in her high heels. The sparkly earrings felt dull as her eyes and her shoulders seemed to be curving downward as though she were a coolie trotting with too heavy a burden.

The beanery that she stared into seemed to invite her with its white tiled floor and scrubbed booths. She needed to sit down and mull over things a little. But most of all, she needed someone who would talk to her and countermen were famous for that.

Kitty went inside and let herself down heavily into the black vinyl booth. An odor of freshly fried bacon rose from the splattering fat on the grill in the rear.

"What'll it be?" the man frying the bacon called to her. Points of gray hair stuck out from his starched hat and Kitty knew that here was a man who worked hard for every penny and would brook no nonsensical gabble from her.

Instead of waiting till he came to her, she decided it would be all right, just this once, to call her order back to him.

"Coffee and a cheese Danish."

"No cheese, lady. Prune or plain."

"Plain, then. Toasted."

She subsided into one corner of the booth and fingered the polished sugar bowl. It seemed to her that everybody, even at this Godless hour, had something to do.

Everyone except herself.

She drank her coffee and ate the warmed Danish just to give herself something to do. For the first time in her life, Kitty realized what it meant to be floating in a vacuum when everyone else had work to do.

"When do the morning papers come out?" she called to the counterman.

"Maybe six. Depends on the trucks, if they're late or not."

Kitty looked up at the round wall clock. Another hour. She would go through the want ads and find a rich old woman who needed a secretary companion.

At least then there would be someone who needed her.

Meanwhile, she sat it out in the little restaurant as various men came in from Broadway, had breakfast at the counter, and left without giving her more than a passing glance.

Kitty thought for a moment that she must be loosing her looks. But memories of Mark reminded her and bolstered her spirit. He wouldn't have bothered with her at all if she were a hag.

The thought of Mark brought her back to Dirk and Dirk led her back to Fred and in memory, she catapulted off to the days of love and promise, so many years ago, when she had dreamed of marrying Fred... dreamed of a buoyant future full of life and children and love and all the good things. Like one long Christmas day, she had dreamed life would be. He had worked at a filling station then and his thick arms were always full of grease when he held her. She remembered the gasoline odor on his clothes and how it had stimulated her with the expectation of wonderful nights.

Fred had wanted to buy his own place, after he finished school. There had been a deal in South Dakota that interested him.

But Kitty had refused to go so far from home and from Rose, already settled in Long Island and pregnant with her first.

As Kitty finished her coffee and ordered a second cup, she wondered if South Dakota would have been any more lonely a place than New York at five-thirty in the morning.

She had to wait till seven for the *Times*. By the time it reached the stands, the wide thoroughfare of upper Broadway had begun to come alive with cars and people heading into the train station and gathering in loose groups for the bus.

As she stood waiting at the corner newsstand, Kitty felt that all she needed was a little perseverance and a little optimism. Her future couldn't be dismal if she refused to permit it to be. If Dirk had been a losing proposition for her, there would be others ... in time.

And besides, Kitty thought as she opened the paper and scanned the Help Wanted pages, if she got a job with a rich old woman, opportunities would open for her automatically.

Carefully she perused the scant columns, making herself remember that this was a week day paper and that if nothing showed up today, she would be bound to find something in the Sunday listings.

Lady wants lady ... .

Kitty tore out the quarter inch of printing and took it with her into a cafeteria in search of a phone booth. It was far too early in the morning to call. But she wanted to check the location of the exchange to discover if it were in the right neighborhood for her purposes.

The listing told her that Mrs. Bennett lived on East End Avenue and Kitty smiled to herself with a catlike pleasure. The cafeteria seemed suddenly bright and cheerful and her eyes became curious about what was steaming in all the metal trays behind the serving counter. After all, coffee and a Danish hadn't been much of a breakfast. She would need all her strength.

Bouncing jauntily, enjoying the click of her heels on the hard, slippery floor, Kitty took a tray and slid it along the tubular rails, capable of devouring everything in sight until nine o'clock came around so she could get herself ensconced with Mrs. Bennett.

Now that she felt better, the faces of those buying breakfast around her seemed to open toward her like morning flowers.

A young boy, not more than seventeen, winked at her from beneath a checked cap. It was an obscene suggestion, really, but Kitty felt glad even for this. She needed assurance that she still looked good. And what could be more direct a judgment than the spontaneous reaction of a teen-ager?

Devilishly, Kitty winked back, then flounced on with her tray to a table.

She poured thick, sweet syrup over her French toast and watched the butter slide around.

"Hi, chick," a voice said and she saw that the boy was sitting down opposite her with a chicken salad sandwich and a glass of soda.

It was daytime and they were out in the open. Kitty felt secure.

"Hi," she said.

Her open reply seemed to startle him and he pulled the cap down lower over his bushy black eyebrows.

"Pass me the salt?" he said.

He could have reached it himself without any effort, but Kitty took it from beside the napkin holder and slid it across the table, feeling herself very much in the spirit of the young and the daring.

She watched him salt his sandwich with a heavy hand and she began to cut into the syrup logged toast, glad that her trim figure could afford the extra half pound this breakfast would put on.

Listening to the sound of lettuce crunching in his mouth, Kitty knew that this boy was all bark and no bite. He reminded her of herself ... as she had been yesterday and all the days before that. Whistling in the dark ... making lots and lots of noise ... but always helpless, always wanting someone to come and rescue her.

Well, she didn't need anyone any longer.

She was about to rescue herself by learning, at long last, how to swim in the deep waters of experience. Instead of closing her eyes and waiting for the waves to rise and swallow her, she intended to watch them carefully, time her move, and float to the top.

Maybe, if all went well, she would never have to get married again. At least not for money. If anything, she would marry for love someday. Pure, honest love.

She ate her toast and let her thoughts roam ahead to those bright times when, independent of need, she could select a mate and live happily ever after.

At a quarter of nine, she left the cafeteria and the boy and took a bus cross town. The few dollars still remaining in her purse might be needed for unexpected eventualities. And the joint bank account she had with Fred could not be counted upon for long.

For all she knew, he might have blown his stack yesterday and withdrawn the balance to leave her high and dry.

Incredulously, Kitty surveyed the shaky earth on which she had been standing all these years and wondered how she had managed to survive this long. The bus bounced along and sailed through the curving path of Central Park and she looked out at the patch of greenery warming in the morning sun. Beyond it she could see the spires of midtown Manhattan standing high with promise. You had to be tough to last in this town, she thought. And she meant to be just as tough as necessary.

Through the heavy traffic of Eighty Sixth Street and the congestion of Park, Lexington and Third, Kitty stayed wrapped in her dreams.

"Last stop," the driver called. His voice wakened her and she got out onto York Avenue to look around and fix her bearings.

She ought to phone from here and then go up, rather than merely arrive without an appointment.

Mrs. Bennett's voice sounded to Kitty like the typically sweet old lady who should be growing begonias and reminiscing about her grandchildren's early birthdays.

Kitty didn't know what she had expected. Something crisp and out of a finishing school, perhaps. Something cooler and more judgmatic than this indiscriminate warmth.

When she hung up, she realized that the muscles above her hips were relaxing.

There was nothing to be afraid of. All the knots that had tied her down were coming loose now.

And soon she would be able to face Fred on her own terms to make an adult arrangement for their permanent separation.

CHAPTER SEVENTEEN

The apartment house where Mrs. Bennett lived overlooked the East River and Kitty paused for a moment to look out at a cabin cruiser tossing foam from its blue white prow.

"Beautiful day, Miss," the doorman said.

"Yes, beautiful," Kitty replied, going inside.

The elevator man took her up to the eighteenth floor and directed her to Mrs. Bennett's apartment at the end of the hall.

It was an old building with mellow tan walls and plain, dark blue carpeting.

The maid who opened the door led Kitty into the calm grandeur of high ceilings and French Provincial furniture that fitted well with the over-all atmosphere of the building.

Kitty waited for Mrs. Bennett in a room of many windows that looked out over Long Island City and the lengthening coil of gleaming river far below. From this height, she sensed that nothing could touch or harm her. The noises of the city were gone and a pleasantly seraphic peace brought composure to her tired nerves.

She heard a door open and Mrs. Bennett wheeled herself in to face Kitty.

Her legs were covered by a Scotch plaid lap robe and only the pointed tips of polished black shoes poked out from beneath.

"Good morning, my dear," Mrs. Bennett said in that same sweet voice.

Pale blonde hair fell in little curls around her crinkled face and dark blue eyes smiled kindly.

"Sit down, won't you?" Mrs. Bennett gestured with a heavily ringed hand, indicating that Kitty should make herself comfortable wherever she pleased.

Kitty sat down into the nearest tapestry upholstered chair.

"It's a gorgeous view, isn't it?" Mrs. Bennett said, following the direction of Kitty's last glance at river and skyline. "I've lived here for forty years and it's still the first thing I do in the morning."

"Anyone would," Kitty answered, wondering what to do, what sales talk of herself to give.

"You saw the ad this morning?"

"Yes."

"I've been running it for weeks." Mrs. Bennett wheeled herself around and took a hard-candy ball from a dish of them. "Women come to see me. All sorts of women, you know. Young ones, older ones. And then they go away."

Kitty couldn't help revealing her surprise.

"Oh, yes," Mrs. Bennett smiled and the brightly colored lips drew back to reveal an untroubled sadness. "What I'm asking, you see, isn't an easy job. Nor too pleasant, I suppose."

"Just what are you asking?" Kitty said, allowing her curiosity to form into words.

"Come with me and I'll show you."

Kitty followed the wheel chair through the rooms.

"I'm taking you on the grand tour as we go," Mrs. Bennett chatted on. "For, if you decide to stay, you'll have the full freedom of the house, of course. And the cars. We would like to find someone who ... who we can think of as a daughter, you see."

"That's asking a great deal," Kitty said.

"I know. But it's been my experience that there's always someone for everyone. Here we are now."

It was the sunniest room of all, brilliantly lit by a single window wall, and Kitty had the sensation that she was floating in the sky. An odor of airplane cement tickled her nostrils with its pungency.

"This is my son, Elgin," Mrs. Bennett said. "Elgin, will you look up for a moment?"

Elgin lay propped against three thick pillows and Kitty realized that he did not have the strength or the muscle coordination to sit up without them. He might have been a good looking boy. A stronger version of his mother, his hair fell in burnished gold strands over a suntanned forehead and the blue eyes, not quite vacant, were flecked with bits of green. Dark curly lashes fringed the eyes and lay half closed as though Elgin were permanently on the brink of sleep. Lush, full lips quivered in recognition of his mother's voice and the head turned ever so slightly, as though rotating on rusted hinges.

"This is Kitty, Elgin. Say hello."

"Hello."

"Hello, Elgin."

She wanted to go to him or do something other than stand stiffly by. But she couldn't judge how much Elgin understood or what would be best under the circumstances.

"Kitty?" he said.

"Yes, my name is Kitty."

"Kitty what?"

"Miner."

Mrs. Bennett's voice interrupted. "Would you like to stay and have a chat with Elgin while I see to some matters in the library?"

Kitty realized that Mrs. Bennett was being polite. She could end it all right now by refusing to be left here with this invalid about whom she knew nothing. A brief flare of anger lashed through Kitty. She told Mrs. Bennett with her eyes that this was unfair. She did not know anything about this boy or what was the matter with him. How much could he understand of their conversation? Or was his condition merely physical, trapping inside the deteriorated body a brain as good and as normal as her own?

But she put a leash on her temper. If Mrs. Bennett hadn't prepared her, she couldn't blame Elgin for it.

"Yes," Kitty said.

She dismissed Mrs. Bennett from her thoughts then and turned to the boy on the bed and saw for the first time a darkish stubble on his face that told her he was not child, but a grown man.

"Does someone build airplanes here?" Kitty said when Mrs. Bennett had closed the door.

"My cousin John."

Speech for Elgin was obviously an effort and Kitty knew that she would have to carry the brunt of the conversation.

"My brother used to build planes," she said. "Solid models, I think he called them. We had dozens all around the house."

"John makes flyers. Flies them from that window. I like to watch … them … go."

Kitty nodded yes. She could see how he would like to fly out of the window as a plane might. Fly out and never return.

"I'm an only child," Elgin said, moving his hand slightly on the blanket. "A change of life baby."

Kitty glanced at him and saw something lively come into his eyes, but die again like a damp match that flares, then sputters out. She went to the curtains and found the cabin cruiser just disappearing around a curve in the river.

"I'm twenty eight," Elgin continued. "About your age?"

"Yes."

She turned to Elgin and felt a smile beginning in the pit of her stomach and rising all the way to her lips. He was as right in the head as any man … and lonelier, perhaps, than any being she would ever meet again.

"If you'd like," Kitty said, "I could come see you often."

Elgin's lashes flickered. "We could get along," he said and with a heavy, tremulous sigh, his eyes closed, leaving Kitty to silence and her own terrible thoughts.

She left the room to wait for Mrs. Bennett in the parlor, but found the woman already there, waiting for her instead.

"I'll tell you something," Kitty blurted. "Your ad said absolutely nothing about what you need here and that's why all those women walked out on you."

She didn't bother to control her annoyance and took out a package of cigarettes to light one with trembling fingers.

Mrs. Bennett moved an ash tray to within her reach.

"Yes, I know," she answered mildly. "But if I had worded it with so-called justice, who would come at all?"

"There are trained people for such work," Kitty said. "Therapists or whatever they're called. You could afford to hire one, I'm sure."

"Certainly, but I wasn't looking for a professional. Elgin may be an incurable invalid, but he is still a human being. He needs that certain … touch, my dear Mrs. Miner. Need I tell you that?"

"No, don't tell me anything," Kitty said brusquely. "I wouldn't know what to say anyhow."

"Then I take it you refuse me," the woman said briskly.

"I didn't say that," Kitty blew smoke furiously. "You and Elgin are two different matters. For his sake, I'd like to try. But only God himself knows what I can do to help."

CHAPTER EIGHTEEN

Kitty promised to move in the very next evening.

She promised ... and she knew that before she did anything else, she would have to see Fred and tell him. Square with him, so that he wouldn't barge in on her one day and ruin everything.

Kitty left the Bennett household thinking, not of her own safety, but of Elgin. There was something about his helplessness that had struck home. Something that reminded Kitty of herself, in a strangely distorted way. But one thing stood clear above all else. She needed to be with this man. Needed to make contact with him. To extend her own life to touch his. Needed to lift him somehow out of the bed of his physical disabilities and upward to where life was, to where hope could blossom, even for the likes of Elgin.

Immediately, she went back to the hotel and checked out, putting into her car only a few of yesterday's wild purchases.

The woman she had been seemed suddenly to have died and in its place had come a burning need that gave her strength. She got out onto the highway and drove rapidly toward the house which Dirk would soon be renting. Even the episode with him, those lurid moments of abandon, seemed to have happened to someone else.

Ringing the doorbell, Kitty prayed that Fred would be home so that she could have it out with him and be done with it.

He came to the door and opened it.

His face, all stubble, his uncombed hair told Kitty that Fred had been indulging himself. She knew how he hated to shave. Without a job to compel him and without her around to nag, Fred seemed somewhat more like the animal she had fallen in love with so many years ago.

"So, the prodigal returns," he said. "Come in and rest the weary feet."

Strangely, his voice did not seem either angry with her nor overly glad at her return.

Quietly, Kitty entered what had once been their home, but was now a disorderly mess of clothing dragged from closets, old baseball gloves, fishing tackle tangled on the dining room table.

"As you can see," Fred began, "the world spins on without you."

"Yes," Kitty said in a subdued tone.

She did not quite know what to do with herself or how to approach Fred.

"Let me help you," Fred continued, reading her thoughts. "You see, I keep up with the news. By proxy of course, but accurately enough to know what I need for my purposes. You spent your first night with Rose and went from there to a hotel, right?"

"How did you know?"

"People phone to keep me posted. Some have more consideration for a man than his own wife has."

"I'm sorry, Fred."

"Oh, don't exert yourself," he said amiably. "I got the message. And since you want to leave me so badly, what the hell brought you back?"

"I didn't come back, Fred."

He started to unsnarl some twisted lures, then carried them to a chair and sat down, as though Kitty did not exist as more than a gnat buzzing around his ears.

"You came for money, then?"

"No, not money either."

"What? Times have changed."

Kitty realized that he didn't believe her. That Fred thought she was stalling for time, to put him in a good mood. She smiled to herself, realizing how Fred really had known all her habits and had let her get away with them. She had never been as subtle or as devious as she had thought.

"I came here to straighten out a few details," she said, pairing two handball gloves and slipping them into an open overnight case. "I assumed that you would like to know where I am and what I'm doing ... in case of emergencies."

"You could have written that in a letter."

Kitty came over to him and sat down on the edge of a hassock. "I don't blame you for any of your feelings," she said gently. "You have a perfect right to be disgusted with me. I'm pretty disgusted with myself."

"Times change indeed," Fred echoed himself.

But he still sounded too staunch, too unyielding

"I hope you'll believe me, Fred. I've been a terrible drag on you for too long. And by rights, it should have been you who left me."

"Truer words have never been spoken," he signed without looking at her.

She reached up and put her hand over the gaudy red lure. "Please," she said, "I'm not trying to wrap you around my little finger. I'm trying to explain."

Fred sighed again. He dropped the knotted bundle to the floor. "Look, let's face it. I don't want you or your explanations. I've had enough. Just pack your little powder puff and blow away. For seven years I've been struggling like a jerk to make you happy. And now I realize that nothing on God's earth can do that, Kitty. You're a malcontent and a complainer. A man would have to be nuts to try to make a go of things with you."

Kitty put her hand on his knee in an effort to soothe the leashed anger trembling through him. She realized that he was struggling not to say it ... that he must know about her night with Dirk. Instead, he had simply dismissed her and her very presence here was both a bore and a bother.

"I'm not arguing," Kitty said. "I've been the worst and I know it."

"Don't butter me up, Kit. I've had it."

She stood up. "I see there's nothing much to say. You don't want to listen ... ."

"Right. Now, scram."

But she could not go. Not like this, with all their good years dangling out on a limb. End it, yes. But nicely.

"If you'll just give me five minutes, Fred. Make believe I'm a stranger and listen to me for five minutes. That's all I ask and I promise you there'll be no requests for money nor for an extension of your sympathies. Okay?"

Fred shook his head. "I'm deaf, dumb and blind where you're concerned."

When he was stubborn, there was no way Kitty could climb the brick wall.

"All right, then," she said, taking a slip of paper from her skirt pocket and scribbling Mrs. Bennett's phone number. "If you ever change your mind, you can reach me here."

She tried to give him the paper, but he waved it away. Instead of letting it flutter to the rug, Kitty put it on the table and placed an old pair of his tennis shorts on top.

"Goodbye, now," she said and left the house.

Sitting in the car, Kitty watched the windows of the house, feeling uncertain whether to drive away or to wait awhile and try again. She felt oddly pleased that Fred had stood up to her. If he could be this strong, this unyielding, she could feel confident that he really would fight his way out of the dull routine into some challenging work that would use his manliness.

To Kitty, this was a revelation. She looked at the tree above as though seeing spring clearly for the first time. Then she blew a kiss to the empty windows and drove back toward Manhattan.

As she drove and thought back over what had transpired, Kitty felt that she had to discover just how much of the sordidness of her past few days Fred actually knew.

Without coyness, she marched into Dirk's office and found him putting syringes out on a towel.

"We're feeling better today," Dirk said, glancing at her, then going back to the glass cylinders, aligning different size needles with various tubes.

"Better and lousier," Kitty said, feeling a strong desire not to mince words with Dirk. "Have you spoken with my husband?"

"Yes."

"When?"

Dirk leaned back against the instrument cabinet and surveyed her with a calm, searching stare. "What's got into you, young lady?"

"Oh, cut out the bedside manner, Dirk. You know what I'm asking. Now, give me a straight answer, please."

"What, exactly, are you asking?"

It seemed suddenly quite clear to Kitty that Dirk would have to be a fool to have told Fred what she had suspected. It could do no one any good .... and all three of them tremendous harm.

"I'm sorry," Kitty subsided.

"Don't mention it."

"It's just that I've come from spending the strangest day of my life."

The crest of energy on which she had been travelling seemed suddenly to ebb and Kitty sat down with a flop in the nearest chair.

"Tell me about it while I'm packing," Dirk said.

Glad for the opportunity, Kitty described Elgin and her reaction to him. Then she spoke of Fred and how he had behaved toward her. Nothing seemed quite to make sense and her own responses were like those of a stranger, as though someone had gotten inside her and switched the wires of her reflexes.

"But I don't need a drink, if that's what you're going to suggest," Kitty said hastily to ward off anything that might lower her guard again.

Dirk laughed with audible pleasure.

"I wasn't going to say that at all," he replied. "I was simply going to ask you to have dinner with me. Growth and change are good, but hard on the nerves. Especially at the beginning."

"But what's the matter with him?" Kitty persisted.

"Who? Elgin or Fred?"

Kitty glanced at him an exasperated smirk. "You think you're a smart one, don't you?"

"Maybe," Dirk grinned. "Maybe not."

Kitty realized that this was no time to try for a diagnosis of Fred's new behavior toward her. Maybe, in springtime, everything blossomed.

"All right," Kitty said. "Take me someplace that'll relax my mind."

"Like the movies?" Dirk said, helping her back on with her coat.

CHAPTER NINETEEN

Well, I have to sleep somewhere, Kitty thought Why not with him?

But she meant to stay at Dirk's place and get a good night's sleep … and nothing more.

They were sitting in a quiet bar that Dirk had chosen, with wood panelled walls and one single, heavy chandelier dispelling a soft light. It was a good place to rest after a hard day's work. A place to pull the pieces together and refresh for tomorrow.

"You know, Kitty, I think you're changing before my eyes," Dirk said, signalling to the waiter for another round of drinks. "Yesterday you were a pampered child, cranky and mean. Today …. Well, today you seem like a grown woman."

"Your surprise is no compliment," Kitty smiled, waving away his offer of a cigarette.

"Usually," Dirk continued, "progress is made by taking three steps forward and two back. I hope you'll remember that when you begin to feel the walls shake, Kitty."

"Walls? I have no walls," she sighed, thinking of sleep and the release it would bring from responsibilities. "I'm all keyholes, you see."

"Peeping through?" he said. "Or waiting to be seen through?"

"Both," Kitty said. "Will you take me home soon, Dirk, and let me go to sleep? I'm dead tired."

"Right now, if you'd like."

"No, have your drink first. I don't mean to spoil your evening."

"You aren't spoiling it, my dear, you're making it."

She heard the enthusiasm in his voice and Kitty felt glad that they had met and were becoming friends, in a strange sort of way.

"I don't know what to make of you, Dirk," she said, playing with her own drink. "One minute I think you're my biggest enemy and the next .... Well, I always seem to be running to you for advice."

"Means you trust me, that's all."

"I suppose I do."

It felt good to trust someone, Kitty realized. She hadn't for the longest time and it felt as though she had been watching people from behind barbed wire, imprisoned in her own concentration camp that allowed no one outside to enter and prevented her from getting out.

Now the wires seemed to be tumbling down. She felt herself moving within a new freedom.

"I want you to like me, too," she said softly. "I need someone, Dirk, and I can't help feeling that it must be you."

"Even though I'm cold and inconsiderate?"

She smiled ruefully at his easy grin. "Did I say that?"

"I think it was sometime last night," he said. "Or maybe more than once."

Kitty shrugged and let her embarrassment show. "I've been known to make snap judgments," she said. "Or maybe you were aloof and inconsiderate."

"Maybe I was."

"Maybe I was nasty," Kitty said in response to his tone. "God, when I think of all the things ..."

"Don't think, then," Dirk said, leaning back and spreading his long fingers on the table cloth. "Come on. I've had enough of this place, too."

They rode back to his office and he took her into the apartment that opened off from the consultation room.

For the first time, Kitty saw unmistakable signs of Dirk's past. A photograph of his father and the medical diplomas surrounding it explained to Kitty that this office had once belonged to another Dr. Dirk Thornwald.

"He passed away six months ago," Dirk explained, "and I'm sort of tending shop till another man buys his practice."

"And you? Why not you?"

"Dad was a specialist," Dirk said. "It's not my line. I want to stay with general practice because there's still a need for that old style country doctor."

"Yes, I think so, too," Kitty said. "Just try to get a doctor in the middle of the night where I was living and you could die first."

The bedroom, a simple room with a large, high bed, looked inviting. Kitty sat down on the mattress and felt herself sinking deep into its springs.

"Feel good?"

"Marvelous," she said, leaning back. "I hope you don't mind if my conversation gets woozy."

"Be my guest."

Suddenly, she hadn't the strength even to undress herself and she closed her eyes, hovering between sleep and wakefulness as Dirk took off his clothes and hung them up.

"Come on," he said. "Move so I can get the spread off for you."

Kitty grunted and rolled over. She felt Dirk's hands pulling the bedspread from beneath her weight and then his fingers pulling off her shoes. The attention felt delicious and Kitty gave herself sleepily over into his care.

Next she felt him unzipping her dress along the curve of her hip and shimmying it up and over her head. He turned her on her side and unhooked her brassiere, then pulled off the rest of her underthings.

She lay nakedly free on a cool blanket cover, feeling clean air wash over her skin. His hands massaged down the muscles inside her thighs and past her knees to calf and ankle.

"Feel good?"

"Mmmm."

Yet even in sleep, her nerves began to respond. She had not wanted this, yet it seemed that Nature knew a more restful cure than mere sleep.

Moving in response to its call, Kitty's hand began to fumble along Dirk's body, searching for his manliness. Idly her fingers began to play, moving against him, circling, till she felt him respond.

"You like it, don't you?" he whispered.

Kitty knew that she need not answer. Her body could be trusted to do all the talking necessary.

As her thoughts drifted hazily away, she caught him and clung with a languid strength, letting the idea of him seep through to stir her desire.

The bed creaked and she knew that Dirk had crept in beside her. His knee moved along her leg and upward to become a saddle. Instinctively, she began to ride it, gyrating her hips without making too much effort. She wanted to remain passive and not disturb herself. She needed to be taken as she floated on the surface of a dream, to be satisfied without participation, as though by a magic wand.

She felt him moving down along her body and she tensed expectantly, waiting for the caress of him that would ignite desire to a bursting flame.

He poised and then plunged and Kitty gasped, arching toward and away from it at the same time, aware that ecstasy would require her to come fully awake at last.

"Go slowly," she murmured. "Make it last …."

Cupping his head, she moved it at the tempo that pleased her. She held him tight against her, as though he were digging a trench into which he would ultimately dive.

"Let me feel you …."

The lankiness of him twisted around, so that she could touch again the part of him that really mattered.

And so what if she were really a whore at heart?

Kitty's mind, filling now with guilt, could do nothing but remain helpless. Like Elgin. Lying in bed, dreaming for something better that remained always beyond reach. She wanted, in her heart, to be lily white with a face as open as a Red Cross poster.

But it would never happen.

The lush fulness of her body needed nourishment or it would die away. And she clung to this nourishment, hard and hot and eager to feed her.

She thrust him suddenly downward and raised her hips to help as he pressed on.

Make it last, Kitty thought. Make it go on forever.

But her wild body craved immediate fulfillment and arched with a gyrating speed as though she were running wildly down a hill of ice, slipping and sliding and unable to stop.

The long line of her body pulled taut as wire and quivered on the point of ecstasy.

"Go on," he whispered. "Let it happen."

A great wave of convulsions flowed through her and she felt the simultaneous pulse of him, while their bodies clung and rolled over the blankets.

Afterward, she lay half off the bed, listening to the sound of shower water running hard in a distant room.

Lighting a cigarette and fully awake now, Kitty stared at the ceiling and wondered what it was about her that always came back to the same low level.

She had had such good intentions. And they had fallen away to dust.

Why?

And wouldn't Mrs. Bennett discern this savage part of her and find it dangerous to allow her to be in the company of her son?

"Am I a monster?" Kitty said when Dirk returned, his hair still dripping water down his forehead.

"Why do you ask such a ridiculous thing?" Dirk said.

"Don't answer a question with a question," Kitty snapped impatiently. "I mean, if there's something ... too much about me, I ought to know it, don't you think?"

"Well, I wouldn't say there's any cause for worry," Dirk answered, rubbing his head with a towel.

"It's like the cork's been taken out," Kitty said, not meaning to be funny, but hearing a rumble of laughter far back in Dirk's throat. "After all those years of frustration with Fred, I think I must be running wild."

"Well, even if you are, it'll subside in time. Give yourself a chance, but don't worry about it. Worry's the only dangerous part about anything. You know, like kids who play with themselves and then struggle with the torments of hell afterward. If people could only realize that sexual indulgence is no more or less dangerous than eating ...."

"Oh, don't be ridiculous. You can't get pregnant from eating."

Dirk tossed the towel onto a chair. "You're overtired," he said. "Try to get some sleep."

Kitty lay with her head on her arm and her eyes tightly shut. Just an hour before, she had been half gone with sleep, but now it had chased off, as though never to return.

A moment later, she felt the weight of Dirk's body getting into the bed and the pull of covers as he turned over.

Dirk had sounded off like such a big shot. She wondered if underneath it all, he was really so steady and confident as he seemed.

Slyly, Kitty slid her fingers over the tight muscles of his buttocks and began to stroke him.

"What're you doing?"

"Nothing, Dirk."

But she kept her hand moving.

"Quit it."

"Why?"

"I need sleep too, you know."

"Do you?" She sounded so innocent, so naive as she snuggled closer.

"Now what do you want, Kitty?"

"I was just wondering…"

"What were you wondering?"

"How much… energy a man as young and strong as you keeps stored up."

Dirk sat up. He switched on the light.

"Now listen, Kitty. I know you're scared and I know you need company, but there are other ways to get it than that."

Kitty sat up, too. "Name one."

Dirk sighed as though resigning himself to a long night. "Join a chess club," he said.

"You know what's bothering me, don't you, Dirk?"

"Yes. And I think that after a few month's separation, you'll be glad to run back to your husband on bended knees… if he still wants you by then."

Kitty hit the blanket with her fist. "Why must you bring that up?"

He gave Kitty his cigarette and propped the pillow more comfortably behind his head. "Because you're over anxious. That's all that ails you, but I don't suppose you can believe it."

"If that's the best you can say, go back to sleep."

Dirk smiled. "Thanks. I'd love to."

Kitty threw her arms around his neck. "Don't you dare."

She felt his hand stroking her naked back and closed her eyes. It was all true, but she could not make herself act on this truth. Fred had surprised her by throwing her out and now, maybe spitefully, she wanted him back. She wanted the satisfaction of having him back so that she could throw him out instead.

"What am I going to do?" Kitty wailed.

"Sleep," Dirk said. "And tomorrow morning, swallow your pride and go back to him."

CHAPTER TWENTY

All the while she dressed, Kitty kept telling Dirk that it was senseless.

Fred didn't want her and he was right not to want her.

"After all," she said, "I've been sleeping with you."

"And what's the matter with me?" Dirk said with mock indignation. "Chicken pox?"

He had no intention of understanding her dilemma, Kitty saw, and so she decided to just shut up.

But keeping silent didn't tell her what to do about getting back a husband who ought not to take her back at all, if he were in his right mind.

"You're going to be a good girl and give it another try, aren't you?" Dirk said into the silence.

"Don't read my mind," Kitty protested. "Doctors are always doing that and it gives me the creeps."

"Well, that's only because we all have the same kinds of troubles. The patients may be different sizes and shapes, but the disease symptoms are usually very much alike."

Kitty zipped up her dress. "No wonder no woman wants to marry you," she said. "It would be like living inside a textbook."

Dirk splashed shaving lotion on his chin. "Could be you're right," he said without concern.

"Well, I don't know what I'm going to do," Kitty said finally. "Only one thing's certain and that is, come hell or high water, tonight I'll be with Elgin Bennett or die in the attempt."

"Good for you," Dirk said, kissing her on the cheek. "Now go jump in your car and see if Fred hasn't begun to change his mind."

Because she had hours to spend and nothing to do with them that would distract her mind, Kitty decided that she might just as well take Dirk's advice.

But one thing she promised herself. If Fred started the same old scene, she would walk out on him before he had another chance to throw her out.

As long as she was going to be humiliated, she might as well do the whole thing herself.

When she reached the house, she rang the bell with an insistent thumb, as though already defending her pride from Fred's abuse.

"You again?" he said before the door was halfway open.

Instantly, Kitty turned around and started back to the car. It had been a mistake for her to come here. She must have been insane to have tried it again.

"Wait a minute," Fred called after her. "As long as you came this far, come inside for awhile."

Kitty paused, letting her body absorb the tone of his words. Were they disgusted? Did they sound, perhaps, just a little superior and condescending?

On a deep breath, she turned around and marched back into the house. If necessary, she could always say that she had just come to collect some of her things.

"I don't get it," Fred began once they were both in the house. "First you run away. Then you come bouncing back. Are we playing jai alai or what?"

Kitty had lots of things she could have retorted, but when she opened her mouth, none of them came out.

"I just came to give you a vote of confidence," she managed to say at last.

Fred, obviously startled, scowled down at her. The stubble had grown even stubblier and she could barely make out the angle of his jaw.

"Confidence? For what?"

"Just in general."

"Isn't that a bit late, Kitty? And unnecessary? Or do you like telling fish they can swim?"

"Don't be such a wise guy, Fred Miner," Kitty blurted. "When I came back yesterday, I found out that I liked you. So what's so terrible?"

"You liked me?"

"Yes. Just that. It's different from love, you know. Or sex. It was always obvious that I loved you. I stuck it out for seven years, so there must have been a reason. But only yesterday did I see in you those qualities that had gotten submerged and that I needed in you."

She saw the disgust smear across Fred's mouth. Kitty knew that she was sounding like a stupid ass, yet she had to get it all said. Fred deserved to hear it, whether he needed to hear it or not.

"And I admire you, if you must know," she hurried on, hacking her way through a jungle of mixed feelings.

"I don't must know anything," Fred answered.

The fishing tackle still lay on the floor where Fred had dropped it and Kitty bent to pick it up.

"Have yourself a ball," Fred said, watching her straighten up little things here and there. "Your day to crow is over, Kitty. I'm going out this afternoon to buy part interest in a plumbing supplies company and pretty soon I'll be going on the road to sell. No prestige. Nothing but hard work and lots of grime. So if you came back because you thought I'd be a good thing to start bossing around again, just forget it. And I mean, forget it!"

The movement of his hands made a wall between them that Kitty realized she could never cross.

"I'm glad for you, Fred," she answered quietly. "And I wish you all the luck."

There was nothing here to stay for, Kitty realized.

It was hardly eleven o'clock and a long day stretched ahead till she would go to the Bennett house and establish herself there. And more than ever she was thankful now for Elgin, for someone who wanted and needed her. She needed Elgin, too. And even if things had worked out with Fred, there would have been time, while Fred was on the road, for her to be with Elgin. He had become a part of her life … the final testing ground on which she must prove herself.

Fred simmered down, but only a little. He turned away from Kitty as he said, "I don't need luck. All I need is someone on my side for a change. Like me. I've been so damned busy trying to keep you happy that everything went down the drain, you know that, Kitty."

"Yes, it's true. And I don't want to stand in your way again, Fred. Not ever."

The sincerity in her voice rang out like church bells, loud and clear. Kitty heard it herself and felt glad. She wanted Fred to understand that she meant for him to have his freedom and that she intended to give him access to it, fully and completely. Never again would she interfere in his life. And he must know it.

To steady herself for the ordeal of saying it, Kitty lit a cigarette. It tasted foul. She had been smoking too much lately. All of her was foul in a way and she knew it would take quite a lot of work and much more time till she was the kind of person a man might be proud to have.

"In case you want a divorce," Kitty said, "I think I can help you with it." She studied the embers burning to gray ash, rather than watch Fred's face. "You see, I've been living with Dirk Thornwald these past few days, so it'll be easy for you to have your freedom."

Unable to face him any longer, Kitty fled the house. She wished that the sky would break open and beat rain down on her head. But the sun continued to shine brightly in a cloudless sky.

Leaping into the car, she jolted off into traffic, running from the knowledge that she had spoken aloud, yet suddenly washed clean by her confession to Fred.

At least she had given him a fighting chance.

Homeless and unsteady, she drove pointlessly, feeling that now she had burst through her wall of glass. Honesty had given her contact with the things she loved. Or at least the courage to reach out and touch as she had been able to touch Elgin.

Driving finally to Rose's house, she was glad to find that her sister was home and Mark out of the house.

"I don't really know why I've come," Kitty blurted. "Except that I seem to be making the rounds today." She laughed through her misery, as though part of her stood off watching the action and able to judge it through the calm eye of justice.

"Well, you look a wreck," Rose said. "Let me make you a cup of tea."

Kitty came inside and went with Rose into the kitchen.

"I just couldn't face you that other morning," Kitty began while Rose put up water to boil. "You know my guilty conscience is bigger than my brains."

"Don't tell me your secrets," Rose laughed, "or I might feel that I have to tell you mine."

"You?" Kitty said, startled. "What secrets could you have?"

"Jealousy," Rose said. "I thought I was going to lose Mark to you. Did you know that? And all the while I was trying to act like a loving sister, I was really hating you in my heart."

"Know something?" Kitty said, feeling a vast flow of relief. "I was feeling exactly the same thing. Jealousy. All my life, I've been jealous of you, Rose. You always had the good things. The looks, the money, the successful husband. It seemed to me so unfair...."

"And you didn't see all the troubles that went with this pretty picture?"

"None of it. Just pure, blind, childish jealousy. But that's all over now," Kitty said, musing. "There are people in this world much worse off than we are. And I don't think I'll ever forget it as long as I live."

While they drank tea and ate pieces of melba toast, Kitty told Rose about the Bennetts and her new job.

"… And I left the phone number with Fred, but he won't ever use it."

"How do you know?"

"When a man has had it, he's had it, Rose. I crawled back to him, but it didn't do me any good."

Rose cleared the dishes, then took her sister's hand affectionately. "Well, don't be too sure. Stranger things have happened, haven't they?"

Yes, stranger things had happened, Kitty conceded. But she couldn't find one single reason why Fred should want her to come back.

The afternoon passed mercifully along as Kitty traded secrets with Rose that would make them friends forever.

"Well, it's time for me to go," Kitty said at last. "And it's wonderful to have someplace to go, did you know that?"

Rose nodded. "And if I know Fred," she said gently, "he finds it wonderful to have someplace to go, too."

Kitty didn't answer. There seemed nothing to say.

She rode back to the city, feeling wrung out and ready for a whole new future.

Her appointment at the Bennett place was still more than an hour off, but she decided to arrive anyway. A few minutes more or less wouldn't make much of a difference.

The elevator man took Kitty upstairs without her having to tell him which floor and she felt that already, she had become a part of things here.

"Well, I'm glad to see that you're early," Mrs. Bennett greeted her. "You're just in time for dinner."

It seemed to Kitty that the one thing she could count on in life was her next meal. But she didn't feel very hungry.

"If you don't mind," she said, "I'd like you to show me my room."

She followed the rumbling sound of the wheelchair over carpets and wooden floors, knowing that someday Mrs. Bennett would spend an afternoon telling her the long story of her life. But Kitty understood the gist of it now: There is hardship for everyone, regardless of either money or station.

The last petal of her jealousy fell away as Kitty sat down in the privacy of her room. She wouldn't change places with anyone now. Not Mrs. Bennett or Rose.... No, not anyone. It seemed to her that each person's destiny, though unique, was ultimately the same. To love and to sacrifice for that love.

As she thought this, Kitty knew that she had come to peace with herself at last.

And perhaps someday, there would be a voice on the telephone, an angry, self-righteous voice, saying: Dirk Thornwald? What in the hell did you mean by sleeping with him?

Kitty hung up the two dresses that were all the possessions she had in the world.

A knock on the door interrupted her.

"Yes, come in."

The maid opened the door. She said, "Mrs. Miner, there's a phone call for you, if you want to take in in the library...."